TEASE

LaDawn Black

TEASE

— *Steamy Short Stories* —

One World Trade Paperbacks

Ballantine Books | New York

A One World Trade
Paperback Original

Published in the United States by One World Books,
an imprint of The Random House Publishing Group, a division
of Random House, Inc., New York.

ONE WORLD is a registered trademark and the One World
colophon is a trademark of Random House, Inc.

ISBN 978-0-345-48665-3

Printed in the United States of America

www.oneworldbooks.net

2 4 6 8 9 7 5 3 1

Book design by Laurie Jewell

To all of you that make me laugh
and smile each day.
Thanks for my daily dose of joy.

Esse quam videri

To be, rather than to seem

Contents

TEASE

TEASE Celebrates Fifteen Years as Baltimore's Top Weekly

Brandi Norris, Editor in Chief

Today is an exciting day for our publication! *TEASE* is celebrating fifteen years of serving Baltimore the choicest scoops on arts, entertainment, dining, and lifestyle trends.

When our founder, Brighton Wray, started the paper at his dining room table all those years ago, he envisioned a free weekly news vehicle that people would actually care about, with stories to keep them informed and get them out of the house to enjoy a vibrant city life. Brighton's vision has developed into Baltimore's top free paper, with its circulation increasing each of its fifteen years. Our Web site, TeaseThePaper.com, is the hottest Web site in the city and one of the best ways to find all of the latest news, entertainment, and of course love, sex, and kink that you've been looking for.

Of course, we cannot celebrate *TEASE* and its success without also toasting the tenth year of our surprisingly successful "Hot Sheet." We are always looking for fresh ways to engage and serve our readers, and when an intern complained about how hard it was to meet people in the city, we charged her with the task of creating a small personals section for the next issue. What originated as five ads offered by single staff members has grown into a section of more than five thousand ads per week (print and online) with a waiting list, and there's always a bidding war to get one of the coveted print slots.

Another step toward fulfilling our founder's mission and serving the community's needs, "Hot Sheet" is more than your run-of-the-mill man-seeking-woman, woman-seeking-man set of listings. We pride ourselves on letting you have your say without ad size limits and all the confusing acronyms. If you want it, say it! As long as teasers are of legal age, they can ask for whatever they want when it comes to friendships, relationships, sex, or love. Our editors are given the task to edit only for clarity, not to alter your ads for political correctness. *TEASE* does not discern for its readers what is or is not appropriate!

"Hot Sheet" is an adult playground where your fantasies can run wild. That intern with dating issues now oversees our paper's top revenue generator and Baltimore's premier dating portal.

The *TEASE* team thanks you for all of your support over the years and promises to remain committed to bringing you the best of Baltimore's stories and experiences: incredible, incendiary, hilarious, passionate, and heartfelt.

Destiny

I Got This

Single sista looking to get laid by a man who will not only know my name after, but may want to grab a cup of coffee in the a.m. Not looking to marry, but just want to be taken seriously. Open to all races because, let's be real, if I wait for a brother I might be alone forever. I'm not a hater; I just want the best. I am a 35-year-old journalist who loves reading (trashy stuff), exercising (no budget for a car), and the outdoors (nothing like an evening on the fire escape). I'll admit I'm looking for love but will be happy with just some mutual respect. I'm a damaged sister who is not yet totally broken. TSOOO

There it is—my very own lovelorn ad. You see, this is my heart and how I really feel, but no one wants to hear any of these things. "Looking for love" means looking for a husband. "Mutual respect" means a lot of men have left and not called back. "Thirty-five" means that I spent the bulk of my prime hookup years screwing losers who didn't call back, so now that the proverbial clock is ticking I am looking for the best donor possible. In the end my ad is pathetic, sad, and desperate. However, it is one of the best things I've ever written; it is probably the most honest statement I've made in a long time.

But, as we newspaper folks know, the shorter the better, and a good edit can turn even the most desperate ad into a winner.

> Attractive 30-plus professional woman looking for an adventure of epic proportions. Romantic at heart with a zest for all things horizontal, vertical, and perpendicular :) Craves attitude, aggression, and passion from men of all types looking to try something new with a woman looking to be her personal best. Serious inquiries only from truly available men. No creepers or creeps.

See, just like that, a spinster can be turned into a nymph. That is what I do. My name is Destiny Brooks, and I am the "Hot Sheet" editor at Baltimore's hottest weekly, *TEASE*. Ten years ago I came to *TEASE* for an internship, and after a particularly bad blind date where the guy ate all his food with his pinky and thumb—no other fingers involved, fork, knife, spoon, nothing—I thought there had to be a better way to meet normal folks. My bosses did too, and we've turned that idea into a portal for normal folks to get together, and also paved the way for all types to find what they really want. Somewhere there is a woman who wants a man who thinks thumb eating is okay, and "Hot Sheet" is where she can find him today.

My job is to turn fantasies into reality, desperation into passion, and toe sucking into foot play. I am the gatekeeper to the hottest section of the newspaper, and every Wednesday thousands pick us up to read and reply to the freakiest fetishes and most passionate fantasies. In a few minutes your ideal match can be found in our pages. Yet the gatekeeper has not found her match?

Now don't start feeling pity for me. The truth is that I meet many decent guys. I am an attractive woman with a halfway pass-able body and I get my fair share of attention. But simply put, I find most men questionable. After three years of overseeing "Hot Sheet" at *TEASE* and handling requests from fellas "looking for a friend" to freaks "looking for someone to chain up in my base-ment," I am a little jaded when it comes to what men *really* want versus what they show and tell you on a date. Once I had to call a guy back after he placed an ad online to verify his content. He sounded like such a nice guy when he answered, but then came the moment I dreaded: when I had to ask him whether he meant he wanted a woman to "shoot his foot" or "shit on his foot." He laughed and assured me that he meant "shit"; to shoot him in the foot would be crazy. After a few more uncomfortable laughs and corrections I hung up the phone knowing that some woman out there has no idea that her man likes foot shitting and is hoping she's the woman of his dreams. So you see, I battle the freaks, predators, and masochists secretly lurking in our men. They don't tell you, loyal wives and fantasy girlfriends. They bring it to me by the thousands every week because *TEASE* is their safe place.

Hence I am alone because I can't trust.

I am that sad statistic that you see blazoned on the cover of every black woman's magazine like a war declaration: over thirty, educated, successful, attractive, and never married. The media track us like humpback whales, estimating our numbers and mea-suring our fertility. When I read their articles on black love I think the writers and researchers miss the point. A lot of us are single by choice, not because of circumstance. I look at my girlfriends, and many of them appear happy and have been married for years to men they've loved enough to take a chance on. I also have single girlfriends who are men hunters. They don't feel that their lives will really count until they get the house in the 'burbs with the stone patio, two kids, and trampoline in the back. And then you have women like me, who can't trust and can't get out of their own way. We aren't man- or marriage-hungry because we have learned to live pretty satisfying lives without them. I know it's going to take a lot for me to fall in love, and personally I am too exhausted at the end of the day to put any work into that, so I pass. I don't complain and I don't chase. I am that friend who makes everyone go, "Why is so-and-so single?" and there really isn't a reason other than because I choose to be. But even I get tired of that answer sometimes.

Once again I am sitting in my office about to hit send to forward this ad over to George in layout for final inclusion, and as is the case about every six months, I am conflicted. Do I become my own client, leaning on "Hot Sheet" to bring me a guy, or do I stick to my diet of random dates and wait for them to say one of the crazy-guy keywords—*rough, submissive, mommy, roommate, knots,* or the all-time winner, *free spirit*—all key indicators that he probably has something to hide?

As usual, I wimp out and just drop the email into my saved draft file to send one day, when I'm brave enough to try what has been so successful for others—a personal ad in "Hot Sheet."

Gloria

> My equal let me down. I want someone brand-new who can appreciate a woman with vintage appeal. Let me show you what a woman really wants and hopefully you can give me what I need. Looking for babes in the woods—35 or younger. TS400

'm not the personals ad type—I wouldn't even be reading this if Deja hadn't left *TEASE* on my coffee table—but damned if that ad doesn't sound like me. I too am a unicorn, the woman who people tell you does not exist. My name is Gloria Tulley, and at fifty-five years old I'm still as hot as I was at thirty and have the sex drive of a twenty-five-year-old. I am not damaged. I was married for twenty-six years to a successful businessman seven years my senior and we have two wonderful children. I was happy during my marriage but never satisfied. My husband viewed me as a possession and not a partner. I handled our home, the kids, our friends, and he worked. We were both heavily invested in our children's success, but as they grew older and depended on us less and less, there was little keeping my husband and me together. Most people looked at our numerous homes, charity work, and overachieving kids and thought we were a successful couple. But things at home were just okay, and while most people could live their whole lives in that state I knew there had to be more.

My husband, Pace senior, loved me sort of like you love an old car: the memories make it great but it really serves no purpose for you now. I love him but I am no longer *in* love with him. All of these years he'd feared that I would leave him once the kids were grown. He'd bring it up as a joke at times, that if it weren't for the kids I would have been gone long ago. I reassured him that this wasn't true in the early years, but as time dragged on I realized that once Pace junior and Amelia were gone I'd be stuck with Big Pace. I knew that I would have to escape. I yearned for adventure, new things, and a man who would not just love me but be passionate about me, the way Big Pace had been in the beginning. Love is responsibility, obligation, and dedication; I needed chemistry, excitement, and intimacy, and the sex that comes with it!

Big Pace and I had not been passionate for years. And I just did not have it in me to grow old with the okay when there was still life to be lived outside the doors of our home. My baby, Pace junior, started freshman orientation at Salisbury University one Sunday. By that Tuesday evening, when Big Pace returned from his conference in Florida, I was out of our main house and fully settled into the beach house. At fifty-five, I was starting all over again.

The beach house was my perfect home away from home. It sat on a small inlet on the Eastern Shore. For the last few years I'd been yearning for a beach house, and when Big Pace found out he started a mad search for million-dollar golf-course homes with five bedrooms or more. When I tried to tell him that I wanted more of a weekend cottage with friendly neighbors, three bedrooms max, and a whole lot of old-world charm, he was vexed.

"Why not invest in a property that we could rent out in an area with amenities that will make the house great for resale?" he asked.

"Big Pace, this isn't an investment. This is our family's weekend home for our kids and future grandkids to come to year after year for a change of scenery." As usual, this fell on deaf ears because Big Pace did exactly what he thought best. That was our story. As our years together progressed my voice seemed to grow more and more silent. Big Pace knew what was best for all of us and we had to live with it.

Living in a planned community of seaside McMansions did not seem relaxing at all; just more house to clean, maintain, and worry over. For weeks he sent me specs of new homes or photos of existing ones. I sent them all back with the same notes: too modern, too big, too close to the boardwalk, et cetera. One night while on the computer I found what I'd been looking for: a 1,200-square-foot cottage built in 1923 and restored in 1955 with three bedrooms and one bath with a wraparound porch and views of the Chesapeake Bay. It sat on one acre in a small town called Kinship. I then found a Web site on Kinship and saw that it was one of a few small towns founded by free slaves after emancipation. It had been a successful, self-contained, tobacco-farming town well into the 1950s, until a huge canning factory was built and the farming families swarmed toward its better-paying, more reliable, and less physically demanding factory jobs. When the factory eventually closed, the town suffered greatly. Many families moved away, and those that remained were working hard to bring new investment into the town by hosting historical tours, working with the local university on preservation projects, and creating promotional Web sites for new residents and tourists, like the one I was on. The town was in rebuilding mode, and I wanted to be in on it!

I will never forget the day two years ago when we first drove out to see the cottage. Big Pace was disgusted by the small stores and local-bar atmosphere of Kinship. There were no chains or big-box stores for miles. The post office was a little kiosk in the town's main grocery store. Most of the homes were run-down because the seniors left in the town were unable to keep them up. And even the better-maintained homes had a trashy feel, with above-ground pools, toy-strewn yards, and muscle cars parked out front. I saw these things but remained hopeful that my oasis still lay ahead. The real estate agent told us that the cottage was on a private road away from the main areas of Kinship. It had been owned by an older couple who'd moved out about fifteen years ago to go into an assisted-living community, and their kids were just getting around to selling it. Currently, the agent, Inez, had five similar houses on the market, but this one was the nicest. It was priced right and structurally sound and could easily be cleaned and ready for move-in or totally overhauled into a modern dream. We pulled onto a long, winding, dusty road where the trees shaded us like a magical secret pathway from a children's tale—I was already enchanted. I could see myself taking long walks along the private road and our future grandchildren spending hours exploring in the woods. The road went on for about a half a mile before I finally saw it—a white cottage with black shutters, a wide welcoming porch, and a chimney right in the middle of the house. An old porch swing swayed in the breeze and the sun danced on the front windows. And the front of the house was the best part—the bay. It was just our house and miles of blue ripples. I turned to Big Pace to ask if he saw what I saw, and all I got was the back of his head heading into the house.

The cottage was warm and inviting, from the living room and tiny dining room off the entrance to the bedrooms and huge kitchen in the back of the house, though it was in dire need of a professional cleaning and rehab. I was so lost in my thoughts—what it would look like if we removed a few walls, updated the kitchen and bathroom, switched the layout—I hardly noticed that Inez and Big Pace were talking over in the corner. I heard him saying that the house needed too many repairs and was far too small for our needs. The view was great, but he'd prefer to have beach access. Inez was trying to save her sale by stating that the house was a huge value for waterfront, but Big Pace, true to form, assumed he knew better than she did and said that the house had no resale value, that any dollars put into it would be a losing proposition. For most of our married life this was the way things went. No matter what I wanted, he had the final call; in Big Pace's mind, since he made the money, the decision was his.

Sensing that her hardest sales pitch had fallen on deaf ears, Inez mentioned some newer properties that we might find more appealing. She turned to leave, and Big Pace was hot on her heels to go check out more fitting properties. It was then that I said, "I will buy this one." Both Inez and Big Pace stopped in their tracks. Inez stood nervously in the doorway, pulled between the desire to thank me for getting the house off her hands and not wanting to step into the eye of the domestic storm about to hit. Big Pace stared at me, unsure of what to do or say next. He asked Inez to step outside so that he could speak to me alone.

He searched my eyes. I did not look away and simply asked him, "What are you thinking?"

"That my wife has lost her mind. I am not putting one dime into this money pit."

"That is perfectly okay," I countered. "I am not using your dimes. I have enough of my own money to buy the house, and I'm sure that I could get a loan for the rehab. This is what I want and I am moving on it."

"What money?" he huffed. Big Pace often forgot that I was one of the original investors in the first Tulley's restaurant. Years before I became a mom I was actually a successful financial investor with a local bank. My commissions, coupled with funds from Big Pace's parents, opened the first Tulley's restaurant. Those were the grand years of our marriage, when we both were successful and incredibly attached to each other. When he sold the first restaurant in order to build a chain of revamped Tulleys, I received a really big check that I reinvested to pretty decent returns. But the day that I told Big Pace that I was pregnant with Amelia was the day that I lost my say. I no longer needed to work, and my full-time job became backing him up.

I told him that I still had revenue from my portion of the restaurant sale, and I saw the wheels turning in his head. There was nothing he could do; I did not need his help or approval, and he knew better than anyone that I could handle running a household in my sleep. The cottage was going to be a breeze.

It took a year to turn it into my dream getaway. I was careful to retain the old-school feel but also include a lot of modern-day conveniences, like a first-floor master suite, a sunny kitchen/family room combo, new siding, a refurbished porch and swing, a two-car garage, and a brick patio leading to the water's edge, providing ample space to sit and take in the view. The final touch was to name the property: "Oasis Found."

Big Pace never strayed from his stance that the house was a waste, even when the kids came down and loved the town, and even when our banker happily approved my rehab loan, mentioning that the "Eastern Shore is a hot investment right now." The kids enjoyed the small dive bars and clubs in Kinship and loved to fall asleep on late nights in the patio chairs listening to the birds and crickets. Even Big Pace's parents enjoyed all of the local history exhibits and the small stores for all sorts of collectibles. I enjoyed watching my family bond. We all talked over dinner, hung out on the porch, and really relaxed. My mind was clearer than it had been for some time, and I could not help smiling at what I'd been able to do.

But Big Pace could not just relax and enjoy it. He was upset that he had spotty cell phone reception, there were too many bugs, he could hear the kids talking loudly long into the night through the thinness of the walls—it went on and on. Not once did he say, "Gloria, I was wrong" or even "Good job." Late one night I caught him sitting in one of the patio chairs watching the night sky bounce off the water. It was a quiet time of reflection that I knew was only occurring because we were here in this perfect space. That was acknowledgment enough that the house was worth the investment even to him.

But after that night, Big Pace never came back to the beach house. Whenever the kids and I rode up, he always had something else to do. At first I was hurt, but then Amelia, my more intuitive child, broke it down for me. She said, "Dad has a hard time with female success. None of his managers are women, and the women he does hire are merely window dressing to get more people through the doors. This success is all yours, and he doesn't know how to deal with it."

"This was a home I made for us. He should just enjoy it," I told her.

"Is it really, Mom? Everything about it says, 'Look at what I can do without you.' Dad is not a fool; he knows that once you start branching out you won't stop, and that is going to turn his finely tuned applecart over onto its side."

I saw her point instantly. This house was a sign of my growing independence. No more kids to preoccupy my time. No fear of voicing what I think and acting on it. Hell, I'd even gone so far as to cut my hair short and start growing it out natural because I wanted to try something different. While I did feel the distance between Big Pace and me, I also was more aware than ever that I had to do these crazy things now. Big Pace knew what was coming even if I never said a word: I was subconsciously formulating a plan to leave my husband.

Two weeks before dropping Pace junior off at college, I had quietly packed my favorite things at our city house and started moving them out to the beach house. I visited a divorce attorney to put together my plans. I did not want alimony or anything propertywise from Big Pace. All I wanted was my car and to make sure that my squirreled-away money and beach house were truly mine. I just wanted not to be married anymore, plain and simple. The attorney said that based on what I told him, the monies in my investment accounts were clearly mine, as was the beach house.

The difficulty in this case would be determining what, if any, interest I had in the other Tulley restaurant ventures. I told the attorney again that I did not want anything, but he pointed out that if I was a shareholder, legally Big Pace would have to either buy me out or continue paying me.

"Continue?" I asked. I had not seen an actual check from any of the businesses since the sale of the first restaurant many years ago. The attorney said that I should have been seeing at least a quarterly payment for the last twenty years because I still had an ownership stake. I was a little dismayed but not surprised. Big Pace probably thought that since he paid for everything, he did not have to give me anything. I told the attorney again to look into my items and that the money from the restaurants was a nonissue for me.

That Sunday dropping Pace junior off was difficult for me. My baby was now officially a man and I had joined the ranks of the empty-nesters. I helped carry his things into the dorm, met his roommates, and had a quick goodbye dinner. And as my boy got out of the car and started crossing the lawn toward his dorm, I finally understood: my son was fine, and soon enough I would be too. I drove straight to the beach house.

At home I'd left Big Pace a letter explaining how I felt and why I felt it was best that we were no longer together:

Pace,

This letter is probably one of the hardest that I have ever written. It is time for us to go our separate ways, and I know that in your head you think this has been my plan all along— for me to leave when the kids go. But that is simply not true. We have been on separate paths for many years now, and I guess I only feel confident enough today to make the decision that I should have made many years ago.

I am asking that you not contact me for a few weeks. I need to understand this new arrangement and figure out what comes next. I will be staying at the beach house and the kids

are a short drive away, so I will be fine. I think we both need
time to think about the next chapter of our lives.

I will always love you, but love changes over time. I do not
regret what we had, but it's time to create new memories.

Gloria

Big Pace never did come out to the house to try to win me back
or even to get answers. He waited two weeks to phone me, and he
was very polite; I could tell he was choosing his words carefully.
He told me that he was not all that surprised with my decision,
that he hoped he'd been a good father to our children and not dri-
ven me mad. He said he was not hurt by my decision, that I'd been
building a life without him for a few years now. Big Pace said he
did feel that it was a bit cowardly of me to disappear. He thought
that I would at least respect him enough to sit down and talk it
through, and what about telling the kids?

The conversation ended with fixing a dinner date to break the
news to the kids and to talk about the split of the financials. I told
Big Pace that I already had all that I wanted, but he insisted that
there were things that I needed to know.

Dinner with the kids went surprisingly smoothly. They took the
news easily, with both of them noting that they knew we had
grown apart. Like even the smallest of children, they were concerned about what would come next: Were we selling the city
house they grew up in? Who would get the dogs? And where exactly would they come home to during breaks? We tried our best
to answer these questions and more. Our kids loved us and they
just wanted to know that we still loved them. They left the restaurant together so Amelia could drop Pace junior off at Salisbury
and then do the two-hour drive back to Howard. Big Pace and I
stayed a little later to clear the air over a few drinks.

"Look," he started, "when the divorce proceedings start, certain things are going to pop up, and I don't want you to be surprised. We have been together a long time and we both know that

it has not always been grand. There is someone else, and I know that your lawyer is going to find her."

Honestly, I wasn't surprised. Big Pace often had been distracted when he was around, and when he traveled he was often ridiculously out of touch. I had always assumed there were other women, so I was more than calm as his side of the story unfolded.

Big Pace then took a deep breath. "Here we go. For the last five years I have been involved with a lady by the name of Maria who lives in Arizona. It started as a fling but now is something quite serious. She is carrying my child."

A child? This sixty-two-year-old father of two adults? What type of sense did this make?

He continued, "I am not here to apologize or even to make you feel better by saying how wrong I was. I wanted to be with her, and it works for me, and that is where it stands."

In that instant I could have just hauled off and smacked his ass with the bread plate. He clearly didn't give a shit that I might have felt betrayed or hurt by this. His concern was that I not think I had a leg up on him in the divorce because he was putting all of his cards on the table. After a minute of typical sister girl "oh no you didn't" ideas, earth got back in contact with Gloria and let me know that this was how Big Pace always rolled, straight to the point and with a clear end goal in mind. I had a quick conversation in my head that went a little like this:

Gloria, you have wanted to be free of this man for many years now. He is giving you what you wanted. It is time for another woman to take care of him and for you to start taking care of yourself. Time for you to get it together and find out why the hell he bought you an expensive bottle of wine and is confessing his deepest secrets. Let Big Pace do what he does best— strike a deal.

I sat back in my chair and let him keep talking. He really wanted to make a go of this new situation and he wanted to control how the kids, his business partners, and employees learned about the new arrival. The only way in his mind to do this was to use a mediator and keep things fast and clean. He would give me the things that I wanted, which to him was really nothing at all: my car, the beach house, and of course my investment money. Also, he was offering to buy me out of the restaurants at $2.5 million. I could always retain ownership, but that would involve lots of lawyers and auditors, and neither of us wanted that. Big Pace would also establish a trust fund for each of the kids that would provide for their lives during and after school and a pretty cushy base for generations forward. All he wanted was to dissolve our marriage quietly and work out a good cover story for his current situation.

I tried to maintain a poker face throughout the conversation, but inside I was jumping for joy. This was way more than I needed or even wanted. Big Pace had given me two of the best gifts that night: my freedom and a guaranteed future for our kids. He was free to handle his "situation." I wished Maria well in my head and wondered if she knew that she was a "situation" in her man's eyes. I thought about that for half a second before I squeezed Big Pace's arm and told him that it was a deal and to just let me know what came next. I left the restaurant overjoyed with possibilities. I closed the door to *my* Lexus and drove out to *my* beach house to contemplate how best to invest *my* money.

Mediation was swift and painless. We basically met in a room, agreed to our predetermined terms, and signed papers. A thirty-year partnership dissolved in thirty minutes. When the mediator read over the document finalizing the divorce, my eyes met Big Pace's, and at that moment, for a split second, we were both young again and back on our wedding day looking into each other's eyes, filled with excitement over what was to come. Outside the court I waited for him to catch up to me, and without saying a word I pulled him to me and hugged him. That moment was going to stay in my mind like our first kiss, Amelia's birth, Pace junior's first broken bone, and so many other moments. Shared moments that were special only to us—our tapestry. He pulled away and kissed me on my nose—our special kiss. I looked into his eyes and saw that tears were forming. He ran his hand along the side of my arm and then walked toward his car. I watched him pull off and thought that this was the first time in a long time I'd known that I was special to him, and that gesture in some ways healed the hurt of not knowing for so long.

Life after divorce was an adventure. I traveled with the kids and took a few island jaunts alone. I enrolled in art classes at Kinship Community College to sharpen my rehabbing skills. My little windfall was working overtime for me, and I decided to actually put a small portion of it to good use. The town really needed to spruce up Main Street a bit, so I'd purchased a few of the abandoned storefronts with a plan to renovate them and make them viable tourist spots on the way to Ocean City. On the agenda were a small Tulley's bistro (surprisingly, with Big Pace's blessing), a real post office and Internet café for residents, a high-end spa, and my personal favorite, a museum to the greatness of Kinship.

The museum was first in line for development. Once word got around about it, all sorts of folks were calling or dropping by the house with stories, photos, antiques, and more. I was starting to get a little bogged down with it all, not really sure how to catalog everything or best capture residents' stories. Pace junior suggested that I post an ad at the college for an assistant. I did, and soon resumes were pouring in. I hired a brilliant young lady named Candace, but before she could start, she regretfully had to decline the offer because she received a better opportunity on campus. However, she said that she had a good friend, a sociology grad student, who was excited about the opportunity, and if I was interested, she would place him in contact with me. Although I was disappointed, I was happy that at least she thought enough of the position to come up with a solution. I told her if her friend was anything like her, I would love to put him to work. He could come by the museum in the morning to talk.

The next morning, I sat at the lone table in the museum going over floor samples with Deja, my friend and designer. While I was trying to decide between taupe, beige, and light brown (all the same color to me), she was gossiping on and on about the new families in town and sharing the latest poop about me. Apparently I am a wealthy old hag held together by staples and tape who is too lonely to have her own life, so I have set on the path of improving everyone else's. At least once a week I have to remind Deja that I could care less what people are saying, but Deja was still talking.

Somewhere between Deja's dirt on the cute guy who runs the tavern and the details of her husband Voo's toe surgery, I heard someone clear his throat at the front door. It was a young guy, tall, reed thin, who looked to be about twenty-three or so. He had stylish glasses and dreads cascading to his shoulders. I asked, "How can we help you?"

"My name is Kennedy Jones, and I am a friend of Candace Fortright's. I'm here about the assistant opportunity." I shook his hand and introduced myself. Deja, never missing an opportunity to touch a new man, introduced herself as well and then made a hasty exit to the flooring store to place an order for her favorite shade of tan. I sat down with Kennedy and told him about the position and my vision for the museum. He said he'd been impressed with the whole idea when Candace shared it with him the week before. He was getting a graduate degree in sociology, as Candace had said, and his final project would center on the migration patterns of freed slaves. His goal was one day to work on centralizing the individual family research out there on African American preslavery bloodlines. "Imagine," he said, "being able to know all about your origins, from the plantation that your ancestors may have worked to the tribe that you came from in Africa, just by going on the Web and having it all at your fingers, just like a typical search engine." He talked about building a database and exhibits for the museum, and I was so energized by his ideas that I offered him the position on the spot. He accepted and said that he would meet me the following day to start cataloging what I had.

At nine o'clock the next morning I was heading to my garage to start going through Kinship history. As soon as I opened the door, I noticed a Jeep Wrangler sitting in my driveway and Kennedy standing on the patio taking in the view. Instead of the slacks, shirt, and tie from the day before, he had on knee-length khaki shorts, a T-shirt, and sandals, and his dreads were parted down the middle and ran in two thick braids down either side of his head. His pecan-colored legs were covered in thick black hair and he had a matching set of tribal tattoos on his calves. He was appealing, and the absence of ego made him even sexier. *Gloria,* I thought, *get yourself together and let this boy do his job.*

I called out to him as I came off of the porch, and when he started to head toward me I was suddenly more conscious of the sundress I had just thrown on. Deja wanted me to toss out my "sunmesses," as she loved to call them, but I couldn't because they were so comfortable. And now I felt like an old bag lady standing in front of this young man. Something deep inside wanted to yell, *There is a killer bod under this muumuu.* What was wrong with me? I'd worn this and much worse in front of my son and his friends and didn't think a thing of it. Why was this young man any different? *Easy—he is not your son, Gloria, and for the record you never wanted to trace tattoos with your tongue on any of your son's friends.*

It had been a while since I'd had sex, and toys can only get you so far. Frankly, my new life kept me so busy that dating was last on my to-do list. There had been offers, but none that made me want to postpone my work. Plus, I was afraid that I might lose myself in a man's shadow again, and now I did not have another thirty years to waste. That being said, I *was* hungry for new meat, and a prime piece was on my patio. Kennedy got closer and I had to get my mind right. Sure, he was attractive, but probably a better match for Amelia. This was a bright boy who was going to help me get my business straight.

We worked for three weeks straight in the heat of my garage, organizing, cataloging, and capturing history. Kennedy was great at getting people to donate things that we needed: our specially treated boxes for documents and photos came from some back supply from the Calvert Marine Museum, the video portion of our work was donated by high school seniors as their volunteer project for graduation, and we got a few extra hands to sort through it all from the senior citizens' organization in town. Not only did all of these things aid in getting the museum going, but they also spread the word on what was coming. The town was growing more and more excited over having its legacy housed permanently. Kennedy had already started reaching out to the media, inviting them to get some footage of our process and working the angle of "big-city philanthropist rebuilding small town." At first I was uncomfortable with this, but Kennedy assured me that there was nothing wrong with using my wealth to rebuild. Whatever it took to get people through the doors was definitely worth my time.

• • •

One morning Kennedy showed up early, and when we walked into the garage I was struck that finally there was nothing to do. We'd gotten to the end of all of the items in the garage. What once had been just too much stuff was now a well-organized storage space. We had even been able to identify the content for our first three exhibits.

"Thank you for making the insane sane," I said to him.

"Gloria, this has really been a breath of fresh air for me, and it kept me out of the classroom, so believe me, this has been more than worth my time," Kennedy said as he threw his arm around my shoulder and gave me a quick squeeze. His touch distracted me. Over the time we'd worked together he'd often hug me at high points, dance with me during boring times, or simply sit with me and look at the sky while sulking. He was the first man that I'd ever met who seemed so free to feel.

Standing there trying to figure out what to say next, I blurted out, "So, since there isn't much to do today, maybe we should take a break for a while until we get closer to the opening. I will pay you up till then, of course."

Kennedy shook his head and said, "No, Ms. Tulley, we are not taking a break. There are press and officials to court, and also you need to have a very well-informed staff in a few weeks, and I'd love to have a hand in all of that." Secretly I was pleased that he was not ready to go. I enjoyed having someone to talk to during the day, and I must admit I loved the scandalous looks we'd get when we were in town. When we were alone, it was easy to forget how young he was, he was so smart and witty. If I closed my eyes, it felt as if I was talking to a great man, but when I opened them I saw that he was just a baby and still taking shape.

"Well," I said, "since we have so much to do, let me make us some coffee and we can get started!"

Over coffee, Kennedy wanted to know the real story of how I ended up in Kinship. He'd heard all the rumors and just hadn't felt comfortable asking until now. I gave him the short version: divorcing, remodeling a home, and looking for my next great project. I told him that I was finally happy and at peace. He asked about my kids. He knew Pace junior from school and from working here with me. Pace junior stayed at the beach house a few times a month just to get some downtime from his roommates. I'd watched him and Kennedy talk once and I was amazed that my son, who was incredibly mature and worldly, was at times rendered speechless in his debates with Kennedy. I asked Pace junior what he thought of him, and he said that Kennedy was pretty sharp and definitely a good person for the museum. Pace junior then said, under his breath, "What do you think of him, Mom?" He winked at me and left the room. My boy was no fool; he knew something was going on.

Kennedy then asked about Amelia. I loved bragging about my politically active daughter. "She is doing great at Howard and staying busy. I am somewhat concerned that she is not really having the college experience of friends and fun because she is just so focused on achievement. She is a lot like her daddy, and Pace junior is philosophical like me." It was strange discussing my daughter with Kennedy. It made me feel a little jealous. Had he asked because he was interested in Amelia? I had to step back and play the mom role no matter what little fantasies I might have had in my head about Kennedy. "When she comes to town you guys should meet. I am sure that you two rebels will have a lot in common."

Kennedy smirked and said, "Is that so? We'll see, Gloria. We'll see."

And then Kennedy laid out his story. He was born and raised in Philly. His parents were both civil rights attorneys who'd met in law school at Penn and prided themselves on never moving out of the heart of the city. His house was always a wild mix of cultures, sexual orientations, religions, and the like. He had two older sisters. One was doing the acting thing out in L.A., and the other was a pediatrician in Cherry Hill, New Jersey. His parents loved the law but, surprisingly, never pushed any of the children toward it. "My folks really wanted their work to be an example of how your career can satisfy you financially and also help you shine a light in your community. So I guess my sisters fulfilled that goal, and I am finding my way toward that."

It was interesting hearing Kennedy talk about his upbringing; his love of history came across as he focused on his own tale. He felt there was a lot of money to be made in making African American history easily accessible, but it would be infinitely more rewarding to inform people of their true origins beyond civil rights and slavery.

That afternoon I gave Kennedy a tour of the house, showing him old pictures and the many renovations that I'd made. He told me about his classes and how he was really digging into his thesis that semester, finding himself on a diet of fascinating philosophy and history courses. I told him that I'd been so concerned about having a job after college that I'd taken nothing but business classes to learn the most I could about money and get the heck out. Raised in the foster system and on my own from age eighteen, I hadn't the luxury that he and my kids had to go to grad school or think about finding myself. Luckily, I had done well enough in high school, and I had a decent enough foster family in the end, who before I aged out had gotten me into college. I moved from my foster home to my dorm and from my dorm into my husband's parents' house, so this was the first time I had ever lived on my own. "At fifty-five, I feel twenty-five, trying to figure out how to take care of myself, make new friends, and let's not even start with dating." *Why did I just say that?* I wondered. Why was I sharing something so intimate with someone who worked for me?

"I feel you on that," Kennedy said. "I am twenty-six, and for all my big ideas, I find women baffling. It's encouraging to hear that I may never figure it out." We both laughed.

We sat for a few more hours going over press lists and floor plans. Eventually the sun started going down, and Kennedy needed to make the drive back to campus. Outside the sun was playing hide-and-seek with the clouds, which were the brightest shade of orange that I'd seen in months. "You are doing a good thing, Gloria," said Kennedy. "A lot of people love the concept, and the ones who don't simply don't know about it yet." In the soft light of the sun, his hazel eyes looked gentle and welcoming. Looking at him, I felt hopeful about all things.

"Thanks," I said.

Kennedy leaned in and kissed me softly on the lips. He'd never done that before. His lips were warm and soft. When he pulled away he looked at me for a response, but all I could do was stand there frozen.

"Um, that was nice," was all I could muster up. He bounded down the front stairs and hopped into his Jeep. I watched his tail-lights as they worked their way down the drive.

I spent the next few hours sitting at my kitchen counter going over that kiss. Had I seemed like a desperate old woman yearning to get laid and he was throwing me a bone? Had I made the mimosas with lunch too strong? Could he really like me? Was this just a polite kiss between two friends who'd spent the day getting to know each other? Was I spending too much time thinking about all of this? The only answer I had was to the last question, and it was a resounding yes. I did the only thing I could think of: I called Deja for her take. Once she got herself together and stopped asking if he'd touched my boobs or squeezed my ass, she gave her insight.

"Girl, that boy is trying to let you know that he likes you," she said. "No twenty-six-year-old man, no man period, spends as much time with a woman as he does with you without being interested in her." I didn't think that was the case. He worked for me, so of course he was there every day. Deja then pointed out all of the after-hours work Kennedy spent around the "office," fixing things around the house, or just hanging out on the front porch. He would even give Pace junior a ride out to the house some weekends and stick around all day. I guess I'd just assumed that he hung around in the evenings for a free meal and on the weekends because he didn't have anything better to do.

Deja quickly pointed out, "Kennedy is a single, smart, attractive young man with no woman and no kids. Do you really think he has nothing or no one to do on the weekends? He wants to do *you*, Gloria. Get real."

But that was it. I didn't think Kennedy wasn't attracted to me. Sure, I was older than he was, but I could definitely hold my own against any woman young or old. Prior to moving to Kinship I was a size six and pretty hot. Now, after months of manual labor and finally going back to my natural hair and shedding all the makeup, my body, hair, and skin were all gleaming. I was once again comfortable in my own skin and felt I was at my most beautiful right this moment. No, there was no question that he would find me attractive. I just didn't see why he'd ever pick me over someone his own age—someone he could actually build a life with. My experience had been that most men wanted to take care of and impress their woman, and there was really nothing a man Kennedy's age could do to wow me. Deja laughed when I told her this. My feelings were a little hurt.

"Look, Gloria," Deja said, "you out-mack women much younger every weekend when we go out, so I already know that you can hold your own in the attractiveness department. But I think Kennedy does wow you every day. It isn't his money, status, or experience that excite you. It is his generosity, spirit, and passion for life that floor you. Plus that tight ass just can't be found in the over-forty set." Deja is a fool, but I had to admit, she was right. It was so good to have a man around who could get excited about something, see the positive side, and think about the big picture. I was drawn to Kennedy because he represented what I needed in my life right now—a fresh perspective. "Dammit, Deja. What should I do?"

"First, get off the phone with me because Voo is giving me the evil eye—he wants dinner. Next, call the boy and tell him how you feel. Gloria, you are beyond game playing. If this is what you want, let him know, and if it is too much of a risk and you just want an assistant, then let him know that. You are too old to be sitting around waiting for any man to make the next move. Call him and get the business of your life going." Deja hung up, and I thought about what she'd said. For all of her zaniness, she'd hit this one right on the head. The second half of my life was about owning it, and it was time to resolve this.

I called Kennedy and his roommate said he was not in. I then tried his cell, but there was no answer. I called his cell again and left a message for him to call me when he had a moment and that I just wanted to talk about what had happened that night. As soon as I hung up the phone, I heard a knock at the front door. From where I was standing I could see Kennedy's Jeep parked in the driveway. When I opened the door he just stood there. I moved to the side to let him in, but he didn't move. "Gloria, I won't be long," he said. "I have been driving around for the last hour trying to figure out what to say, and this is what I've come up with. I really like spending time with you. I think that you have so much to teach me, and we share a lot of the same ideals. You are fine as hell, and honestly, I am often distracted. I apologize if the kiss was inappropriate. My intention was never to make you feel uncomfortable. Silly, I guess, but I enjoyed being with you today, and I kind of let my secret desire step into our professional arrangement. I love the project and I want to stay on, but I don't want you to feel strange, so I will go if you want me to. I don't feel bad about what I did. Only sorry if it hurt you."

Here he was, hat in hand, telling me that he wanted me, but more importantly wanted me happy. No man had felt this way about me—ever. "You drove around for an hour, and that's all I get?" I simply could not stop beaming at him. I was smiling so hard that my face ached.

"Yeah, pretty much," he said, standing before me with his hands jammed into the pockets of his shorts and shuffling from foot to foot. He was too nervous and too cute.

I stepped out on the porch and sat on the steps. Kennedy sat down next to me, and I then did what Deja had told me to do, what I had wanted to do with a man all my life—I told Kennedy how I felt. I told him how beautiful I thought he was and how different he was from any man I'd ever met. Kennedy made me nervous and self-conscious in ways that could happen only when a woman is attracted to a man. I wanted him, no question, but I did not want to be the "old-lady experience" for him. I was willing to move forward only if I was what he wanted. I was ready for something—someone—new.

Kennedy turned me to face him and said, "Gloria, this is not a game, and I am not one of those check-off list guys just looking to say I have been there and done that. All I know is that this feels right, and I want to go with it."

When he leaned in to kiss me this time, he was deliberate. He put his hands on my face gently and looked in my eyes as his lips searched out mine. Tears started streaming down my cheeks, wetting his fingertips. I kept closing my eyes to stop the stream.

Kennedy whispered over and over again for me to open my eyes and see how much he wanted me. I looked at him and I could not stop crying and smiling. That moment was cleansing—getting rid of the past hurt and disappointment and looking at what lay ahead. Kennedy kissed away my tears and assured me that I was "going to love this."

I stood to lead him into the house, and once we were standing, Kennedy said, "No. Here." He walked me over to the porch swing. "I have thought about being inside you so many times right here at night with the water in front of us. Let's do it."

I couldn't say no. Kennedy removed his T-shirt to reveal the broadest pair of shoulders I have ever seen. His legs and arms and his chest had just a very fine coat of the silkiest black hair. I am one of those women who love chest hair, so this was a treat. He sat down on the swing as I stood between his legs. Kennedy asked me to undress for him; he wanted to see everything. For all my bragging about my workout routine and about how the guys at the market go crazy over just a hint of my tits, this was hard for me. The truth was I was a very well-preserved woman of fifty-five who'd had two babies. What was this young man going to think of my well-traveled form? He was probably used to belly rings, nipples saluting the sky, and thighs that never said hello to each other throughout the day. A dark bedroom under the covers was safe, but here, so close, with no cover, under the stars . . .

Sensing my apprehension, Kennedy said, "Gloria, darling, I just want to see you."

This was my chance, and I wasn't going to blow it. To hell with the insecurities and what I should do or what other people might think . . . and to hell with that sunmess. I reached down to the hem of my muumuu and lifted it over my head. Luckily I had on my nice lace bra and panty set and not my typical Hanes-variety cotton set. I was reaching behind me to unhook my bra when he stopped me and stood up. He pushed me back and just looked at me there on my porch in my bra and panties. He spun me around and declared me "simply incredible." Kennedy then came around behind me and bent my body down over the seat of the porch swing. My ass was in his crotch and my elbows were supporting me on the swing. He ran his hands along my back, starting at my neck and going all the way down to my hips. I heard his shorts hit the ground and he pressed himself against the fabric of my panties. Kennedy leaned over me and kissed my neck. I felt his excitement growing harder, and I was so wet that my panties were sticking to me. It had been months since I'd been with anyone, and my last escapade hadn't been much to talk about. It was my divorce attorney and it was fast. I had too many drinks to celebrate the settlement, and he was too married for either of us to take it seriously.

But here I was, on my porch swing, with a very naked, very hard Kennedy. I turned and sat facing Kennedy on the swing. His body was something to behold. His skin was smooth and every muscle clearly defined. He walked toward me, caressing his dick in his hands, and asked me if I wanted to taste it, and all I could say was yes. Kennedy straddled me on the swing with one leg on each side of my thighs and held on tight to the chains of the swing. I took him in my mouth, and he tasted so good. I rubbed the tip all over my lips and even down over my nipples. He moaned with every twist of my tongue as the swing rocked back and forth with every motion of my head on his dick. The cool sensation of the night air was making me suck him off harder. I tightened my grip on the full length of his dick with my lips. The vein underneath his penis was pulsing, and I knew I had him where I wanted him. I pulled away to reposition and put him inside me, but Kennedy edged away from me, rubbing the remnants of his love all over the tip of his penis. Right there in front of me he came. It was soon and unexpected, but okay. I simply pulled him closer to me and licked it off his trembling member and held on to his thighs while he caught his breath. Kennedy slid down and sat next to me on the swing. He wrapped me in his arms and kissed the top of my head and said thank you. I kissed him back and bent over to grab my dress from the floor. Kennedy kicked my dress away and said with a laugh, "You don't need that; we are not done. I don't remember you getting yours. And does it look like I am ready to stop?"

I had to chuckle at that because when I looked down he was still hard. Most men I knew could not last through previews, let alone the full show. This was definitely an unexpected double feature.

Kennedy and I went into the house and into my bedroom. He removed my panties and placed me on my back on the bed, saying, "You gave me what I wanted, and I want to give you whatever you need. Tell me, and I will do it for you." There was nothing to say. I wanted it all. I wrapped my legs around his back and let him inside me. His dick made me want to scream his name. It was as if it knew exactly where I needed to feel it.

While Kennedy was inside me, he kissed me all over. He wanted to see every inch of me and know exactly how I tasted, smelled, and felt. As we moved together I grew bolder and more confident. I whispered into his ear how hot he was making me. I held on to his hair while I told him that I wanted him in me from behind. Kennedy flipped me over and I got on all fours. He did not want that and pushed me down flat on the bed on my belly. He said he thought I'd enjoy this much more. He crossed my legs at the ankles and entered me from behind. My pussy felt so tight around his dick, and with his every thrust, I grew weaker and weaker. Sweat started to pour down the small of my back, and I had to reach behind me to hold on to his thigh just to ground myself. Kennedy then placed his hand under me and started playing with my clit. When his thrusts quickened he flicked my clit faster, and soon I was screaming out his name so forcefully that I am sure that it echoed outside. I could not stop shaking, and my body was just a mass of nerves under his. Kennedy lay on top of me, kissing and stroking my hair, his locks pouring over my shoulders. He held me for the rest of the night. Strangely, I did not mind that he took the lead. I felt balanced, and for the first time free to be both vulnerable and strong with a man. In this moment I was his woman and I was okay with it. I was satisfied, finally satisfied. I did not know where this could go, but I did know that with him right then was right where I needed to be.

In the morning, I wanted more of him. I was a little frightened by my passion because it seemed as if I could not get enough. Surprisingly, I wasn't tired. My mind was filled with images from the night before and a lot of "is this really happening" thoughts. After our morning session, we just stayed in bed and talked about what would come next and how best to handle the situation. Kennedy made it clear that he didn't care who knew. I told him that I felt the same way, but I thought it was smart to keep it quiet until the museum opening. All I needed was a bunch of rumor mill fodder over how the owner was screwing her assistant. I think Kennedy understood my point and agreed to it, but I saw in his eyes that he really could care less what anyone thought; he just wanted to be with me.

I gave him a small break to go take a shower and get dressed while I made breakfast. Before jumping out of bed he told me that there was a great spot he wanted to show me later that night, so I should wear something sexy and he'd get me around eight. A real date—I was intrigued.

I heard the shower come on, and I started pulling out the pans for breakfast in the kitchen. Just as I had all of my ingredients lined up I heard a knock on the door. So much for keeping things quiet. I shut the door to the master suite and went to answer it. It was Deja. I had forgotten that we were supposed to go to pick out furniture for the museum lobby that morning. She walked in, shaking her head, and said, "Where are you hiding him at?" Deja ran over to the bedroom and made a play for the doorknob, but I swatted her hand away. She laughed and grabbed a stool at the kitchen counter.

"So I take it the two of you came to an understanding last night," Deja said. I smiled; I couldn't stop smiling, actually. "Let me guess. He told you that he loves old pussy, and then you made your case that this thing was too ridiculous for words and that you both should walk away." I just giggled. There was no stopping Deja when she was on a roll. "But then I guess he was just so heartbroken that you offered him your bed for the night and your shower in the morning to soothe him so that he could work through all of the rejection. Right? Damn it, Gloria, you have such a big heart! I am so glad that you are my friend."

The door to the bedroom opened and Kennedy came out. When he rounded the corner he saw Deja, said good morning, and then walked up behind me and kissed me on the neck. My body tensed, and Kennedy said, "I already know that Deja knows. She knows everything. I promise not to do that in front of anyone else." He asked if anyone wanted some juice and went to the fridge. I'd forgotten to buy juice, and Kennedy offered to go grab some from the market.

Before he left the house he kissed me again and patted me on the butt. I stood there blushing like a teenager. Deja interrupted the peaceful moment when she said, "All I want to know is, was he packing or lacking?"

Damn, Deja. Damn.

Staci

I am your fuck fantasy. Looking to just get on and get off. I need it just as bad as you. I don't want to take long walks or have spiritual conversations. All I need is for you to be willing. Your ultimate experience awaits. TS568

I am a dick connoisseur. There isn't a size, shape, or color that is foreign to me. When I ride the light rail into work I love to sit behind my shades and just stare at the bulges in men's pants. If I see that a dude's dick bends a little too much to the side, I know he's a G-spot man and fucks a lot, hence the permanent bend. If a dude is all bulge right in the middle, then he is all balls and no dick—the balls act almost like a push-up bra on a woman. Probably not a good fuck, but he is probably one hell of an eater to make up for it. Then there are the flat-front dudes. You don't really see anything when you look at them. Those are the best because a lot of times they're hanging low enough to swing freely and offer the most bang when fully erect. I love riding the train!

Black men do have big dicks, but so do white men, Latino men, and probably just about every other group of men on the planet. I have had many brothers disappoint me and quite a few white dudes make me clench the sheets from the power of their sex. All of us true dick connoisseurs know that size is overrated. Other than being something to marvel at, big dicks do nothing for you if the men attached don't know what to do. Women who chase big dicks can't fuck, plain and simple. They go after big dicks so that they can just lie there and do nothing. Side note: these women are usually the ones who will tell you that they have never had an orgasm.

Uncircumcised dicks are the most sensitive, and often these men have the best dick control. When I listen to women talk about how "ugly" and "unclean" they are, I just shake my head and think, *Pick up a book, you dumb bitches.* Uncircumcised penises are often cleaner because dudes have to clean more carefully with their foreskin in place. And sexually they're more sensitive because the tips of their penises haven't been numbed down by years of contact with clothes, sheets, and the like. That ultrasensitivity teaches them to pace themselves more during sex—which means they often go longer and can actually control when and how they cum.

My mind is filled with dicks, and whenever I can be on top of one, in front of one, or even face-to-face with one, I am good. Regular hookups bore me; the whole "getting to know you" routine is tired. Most men, I could care less about their jobs, future plans, or bank accounts. When the hell are we going to fuck? Now, you'd think men would champion a woman like me. No, they don't. Most go soft at the challenge, and those who are game try to turn it into a love thing so that they can lock this good thing down. This isn't about love, it's about release. So meeting dudes the traditional way had to go.

The Internet worked well for a while, but the most interesting guys didn't live in Maryland, and the local ones were usually homebound geeks, predators, or dudes on disability who loved to be freaky with their mouse pad because they knew no real chick would give them any. I had only one real prospect online, but while the dick was great, it had a wife and four kids attached to it, so there was only one meeting.

Personally, my saving grace in my dick pursuit has been *TEASE*. It is the only place where freaks and normal people come to play and you actually get quality hookups. Everybody in the city reads *TEASE*, from the politicians to the barbers, and everyone knows that *TEASE* is the shit for what's hot in Baltimore, so it makes sense that in the "Hot Sheet" section, anything and everything you could possibly want is there: men wanting to lick other men, women craving a change of pace, and even one of my favorite ads of all time, from a knee lover (apparently this dude liked having women jerk him off using their knees). As long as it's legal, it can be found in *TEASE*. So I place an ad every month . . . and my mailbox is always full.

I met one-nut Sean, two-tone-dick Akil, and sock-loving Tarique, who could only cum with a sock on his dick (tube to dress sock, we tried them all). While there have been some characters, they've all given me what I needed—a good fuck—and I owe each four-star fuck to *TEASE*.

Destiny

Working with Freaks

> Grass in my ass is a wonderful thing. A true green dick looking for a very green lady to share outside adventures with. No couples or group sex—just one-on-one activity. TS014

This week was crazy! We published our annual "Freaks on Parade" issue, comprising the wildest personal ads we've received all year. The crazy requests that I get for "women with pot-bellies" or "men with horse balls and tight asses" get their shine in this issue.

My favorite part of our "Freaks on Parade" issue is giving our staff the opportunity to write pieces describing their own fantasies. We dedicated an entire pullout section to a behind-the-scenes look at what the *TEASE* staff thinks about during the day, and I must say our little office of ten is mighty freaky. All of our submissions are anonymous, and I always have a lot of fun trying to guess who is who.

Some are obvious. Felipe, our politics reporter, always fantasizes about a big white guy overpowering him in the lunch room and taking him from behind over the shredder while humming Beach Boys tunes in his ear. His cubicle is a shrine to the Beach Boys' blond, blue-eyed greatness. When guys come to the office and attempt to flirt with him, I just laugh; Felipe is a beautiful Puerto Rican man who only likes blond guys, so even though the ladies swoon because he looks a lot like Benjamin Bratt, and even though the brothers love them some Felipe, they have no chance.

Sol is our crime stat guy as well as the only white guy in the office. Each year his fantasy includes his love of legs. I know this fantasy comes from Sol because he stares at legs all day. The man even positioned his desk chair in such a way that he can view women's legs all day long as their owners pass by his office. Sol's piece lists the standout legs of the year and what he would do with them if he could just touch them. This year they belonged to Heidi Klum, Selita Ebanks, Serena Williams, Gisele, and his standby year after year, Mary Hart. Each year the women change, except for Mary Hart; he loves the glass desk on *Entertainment Tonight* (easy visibility) so much that he suggested we get them at the office. This year he wanted to wrap her legs in string cheese, spray cooking spray on them, and paint them with kids' yogurt; he likes the pastel colors.

Other co-worker fantasies are harder to decipher. This year I had two on my desk that really intrigued me. One was from a female staffer who loves getting it on with strangers in the bathrooms of fast-food restaurants, and the other was a gender-neutral fantasy involving being rubbed all over with stuffed animals—can we say childhood issues! When I look around the office our fast-food humper is not apparent. There are four men and six ladies on staff. I am definitely not the fast-food humper. I'd much rather hook up with a number 10 with curly fries than some highway worker on his lunch break. I want it to be Deanna, our God-fearing, prim-and-proper receptionist from a prominent local family. Every day she comes to work in long skirts and sweater sets and never wears her hair down, preferring to twist it up on her head. Deanna is approaching fifty and has never been married. Her passions are her church, her house, and ministering to the twisted clients of *TEASE*. When ads come over the fax for "Hot Sheet," Deanna turns over the dirty ones and places them face-down in my box. The ones that are borderline disturbing she slides under the blotter on my desk. If a client comes in and asks about an ad, we have fun watching her squirm while the person is trying to explain that the ad said "dick sucker" instead of "dick tucker." We know it can be too much for Deanna, but she stays because she says the office needs her "light." I have never heard Deanna talk about a man, but I have ten fantasies in hand and hers has to be one of them. I can just see Deanna hoisting up that long cotton skirt and letting her hair down in a filthy McDonald's stall with some downtown attorney type because she was turned on by the way he filled his cup with ice.

While Deanna is a funny choice, the hot choice would be Katina. Katina is the type of woman who literally stops traffic. We went to the same college and when she started at the paper as a photographer we fast became work friends. Look, I am a woman and sometimes you just have to give another woman her due— Katina is sexy as shit. Her body is perfect and she is naturally beautiful. Because she is a photographer and a struggling artist, she has a down-to-earth quality that attracts people to her. On her first day at *TEASE* the guys in the office acted like they were back in high school. She'd talk to them and they had to fight not to look at her boobs or watch her walk away. If she was the fast-food humper, these guys would lose their minds trying to picture it. Even Felipe, who probably has never even seen a pussy, said that Katina made him want to go straight for "like five minutes." You know you're hot when gay men want to screw you.

• • •

I decided to do some detective work. I checked out the paper that the fantasy was written on. Just your standard office paper. There were no marks, smells (yes, I sniffed it), or impressions (I watch *CSI*) that gave away who the author may be. Not knowing who wrote it was killing me, and it was a slow day for ads, so I thought up a plan to reveal my humper. I sent an email to everyone in the office stating that the person who'd left the fantasy about passion in the bathroom needed to shorten and resubmit the piece. In my email I said the person could email the change or simply drop it in my bin by the end of the day (hoping whoever it was would do it while I was there).

All day long I checked my email and in-box. Who was the brazen freak at work who liked to kick it with strangers? And where the hell was she having sex? Obviously those bathrooms were spacious and clean, and I needed to know where to go when I had to go. And more importantly, is the toilet paper stand a reliable footrest? The last time I hooked up in a bathroom was six years ago with a college ex in a club bathroom stall. He was fantastic in bed, but the stall was tight and hot and there was a lot of uncomfortable jockeying for space. As I undid my jeans I accidentally bumped against him. He came in his pants and ran out of the bathroom. It was a tragic scene and forever changed the way I viewed stall sex. If there is a sister out there who makes it work, I want to know her secret.

No emails came in and no one dropped anything at my desk. My humper was playing with me and was not going to reveal herself. I even took an extra-long lunch in our break room and watched every person who walked in and out my office, but still no update from the humper. This person would risk not having her fantasy run rather than chance me finding out her true identity.

By the end of the day, I had given up on finding out who the humper was. I decided it was probably better that way because I might look at the lady differently—Deanna wouldn't be so perfect or Katina so earthy. And besides, some fantasies probably shouldn't be revealed because they represent only a small piece of who that person is. I cut my computer off and packed my bag to head home. I was walking back to the break room to grab some leftovers from the fridge when I saw someone approaching my desk. I couldn't see well through the blinds in the break room, and I did not want to peek out and cause my humper to scamper away. It was then that I saw Ms. Ty coming from my office with her duster and sweeper. Damn, it was just the cleaning lady making her rounds. I waited for Ms. Ty to leave because I really wasn't up for a twenty-minute conversation about her daughter's latest "when bad men get worse" drama. When I heard her shut the door to Sol's office and start work in there, I slid out of the break room. I took a quick peek into my office and saw something sitting right in the middle of my desk: a neatly typed update similar to the first submission. My desk had been clean only minutes before. Who'd left the update? Everyone else had left at five on the dot because we'd gotten free Orioles tickets. It was then that I remembered that we had included our cleaning staff on all office email lists since Desmond, our carpet cleaner, killed with ten minutes of comedy at our Christmas party. Was Ms. Ty the fast-food humper? Ms. Ty *is* feisty and fun. But she is also the mother of four adult children and is shaped like Grimace with fake teeth that she only wears on special occasions. If a sixty-year-old grandmother is getting hot sex on the regular, my ass is simply pathetic.

Get the fuck out of here, Destiny—Grandma Ty gets more than you do!

Jacob

I love cheaters. Hitched women are my passion. Looking for a wife to play with. Fun and games with an erotic spin are my specialty. TS210

I love married women. Not only is doing them physically pleasing, but I find their mental game to be tight. They aren't leaving their husbands, and because of all the demands on their time they show up, get naked, get off, and are gone. No ties. Now, some have fallen in love with me, but for those unfortunate few, I had to become a nightmare lover in order to scare them straight—straight back to their husbands.

Like there was Malenga, a fortyish schoolteacher that I met at a restaurant a year back. She'd been married for twenty years and was tired of her husband's constant lies. Her husband had had numerous affairs and Malenga was looking for payback. We met up daily at her small condo in the city after she got off work, the same condo her husband used for his trysts. Malenga felt that since he was out of the country for a month on business with his latest piece that the space should not go to waste.

It was an ideal situation. Malenga was looking for sex and I was providing it, and I didn't even have to break things off in the end because her husband would be home soon and we would have to stop. Hubby came back home, but Malenga did not stop. She called me at all hours. Showed up at my job and even followed me out at night. We had unfinished business and there would not be another guy in her life who just disappeared when he wanted. I reached my boiling point with her when she started actually approaching other women I was seeing and telling them that she was my woman. It was time to flip it on Malenga.

For the first time I invited her over to my place for dinner. After climbing five flights of stairs, she entered my efficiency and sat down on my futon, and I could tell that she was put off by how I lived. I set up the small bistro set in the corner with our dinner and lit some tea candles to set the mood. Once we finished our meal, I sat next to Malenga on the futon and told her that I was wrong to have ignored her and that I really hoped she'd spend the night. She looked around my place again and said that she had to be at work early in the morning, so it was best she left now. She gave me a quick peck on the lips, grabbed her fine leather bag from the floor, and made a mad dash out the apartment door and down the stairs.

Minutes later my boy Colby knocked on the door and I thanked him for letting me use his place. "Did it work?" Colby asked.

"Like a charm, as always," I replied. I learned a long time ago to never ever let a hookup know where you really live because they will always pop up, and there is nothing that will convince a cheating wife to go back to her comfortable home faster than a brief look at her pauper's future with you. I gave Colby his key back and skipped happily down the same stairs that Malenga had used as an escape route minutes before.

In the past my hookups were random: a woman at work, some-one I met through a friend, or even a woman I picked up on the street. It always began the same way: a friendly gesture that led to emails, then long lunches, and finally sex. They all started out saying no and with just the slightest prodding they all eventually said yes. Married women are easy for three main reasons:

1. *They crave excitement and passion.* Their husbands can be physically attractive men, but often they know only one way to hit it and don't realize their wives are bored with them sexually.

2. *Years of hate have hit their zenith.* Many of the women do not like their men anymore. Either they married too young, before they knew what they wanted, or they simply have been too disappointed over the years to have any faith in their man.

3. *They need to feel feminine.* I give them a reason to dress up, work out, dance, and be all things ladylike. Even the dowdiest soccer mom will change her style for a lover.

I am not a charlatan or a home wrecker. I provide a service whereby I reignite the fantasies of the forgotten. These relationships have all the sex and none of the drama of being in a committed relationship.

A few weeks ago I picked up the latest edition of *TEASE* to check on the gig date for my favorite local band and found myself reading "Hot Sheet." I looked over the "women seeking men" section, and an ad jumped out at me from the page:

> Seeking a new thrill. Looking to bask in the youth and strength of a lover. Married lady who is sick of the routine desires a part-time tryst with only the best. Discretion is of the utmost importance—along with a creative mind and a hard body. TS432

I wanted to know more. Having never responded to a personal ad, I didn't know what to expect. Would she be someone's fat and disgusting housewife, or would she be one of the hot MILFs that crawl around the gym and the malls looking for their next prey? For all I knew this could be some wacked-out man looking to kill men who sleep with married women—a love terrorist. With all of these thoughts and much more pouring through my brain, I decided that I would give the number a call. When I punched in her code the warm and friendly voice of the woman who'd written the ad greeted me, read her ad, and then politely asked the caller to leave her a message. I did.

About a week later she sent me an email in my *TEASE* mailbox stating that she liked the sound of my voice and wanted to get to know me better. We emailed each other for a few weeks and then I gave her my cell number. She'd call during the day when her kids were at school or late at night when her husband was asleep. Her name was Delia and she had been married to a government worker for the last fifteen years. They had two children and she was a stay-at-home mom even though there was no one really at home to stay home for because her kids had been in school for years. She used to be an art dealer and we would talk for hours about art and her travels before she got married. She loved her family but had fantasies of leaving them all behind simply to be a free woman again with no responsibilities. Her husband had no idea who she was anymore, and she didn't think he even really cared. In her mind, he loved their easy routine—not her. Delia had stopped being his wife and lover years ago. To test her theory Delia cut her waist-length hair to her shoulders and dyed it red—the same hair that she had been growing out for the last ten years after a horrible hormonal decision to cut her hair while pregnant with her oldest, Jessamy. It took him four weeks to even notice and the only reason he did was because they were at a party with some friends who simply could not believe she had cut her hair. It was then that Delia decided she needed a change and placed an ad in *TEASE*.

I could tell that she wanted to meet me, and I must admit that I was hyped to meet her too. Guys always know when we're intrigued by a particular lady because we'll rearrange our life to see her and possibly hook up. Although her ad was pretty forward, Delia always turned me down whenever I mentioned meeting up for a drink or going out for coffee. I think she was a little unsure if she could go through with it. Once I was so desperate that I said that she could just meet me at the American Visionary Art Museum and we'd check out the exhibits, and if I wasn't her flavor she could disappear into the masses and never contact me again. I hadn't thought about art since the eleventh grade, but if it got her out to meet me, I was definitely down with the visionaries. Delia was proving to be a challenge, but I was willing to put in the work to win!

My life is about making people sweat, and during the day I do that as a trainer at Mission Gym. One day as I was working my client through a series of futile butt-building lunges, I noticed a woman staring at me from the elliptical machine across the room. She was a thin redhead with small boobs and a tiny waist. Our eyes locked, but she didn't look away. She stared at me and smiled and then went back to her workout. I was intrigued and wanted to meet her right at that moment, but my client, Roberta, was breathing hard next to me. I really wanted to tell Roberta that her dream of being bootylicious was just that—a dream—and that she was wasting her $75 an hour, and go talk to this mysterious elliptical lady, but waited it out. Once I was done with Roberta I went looking for the woman but couldn't find her anywhere in the gym, so I assumed she'd left for the day. After a quick shower and change I headed to the front desk to sign out and get my schedule for the next day. There was an envelope in my mailbox along with the schedule. I tore open the envelope and inside was a flash drive with directions to connect it as soon as I could.

I pulled out my laptop as soon as I got home and connected the flash drive. Once the file uploaded I recognized the redhead from the gym. It looked as if she had taken the film with her Web cam in a dimly lit room. It was Delia—finally I was able to put a face with the voice. And what a great face it was. She had porcelain skin covered in light brown freckles and hair the color of strawberries. I could only see her from her shoulders up, but it was clear that she was topless because I saw that sexy line between her breasts contract when she moved. She said she'd come to the gym to see me. She knew where I worked because I had called her from there a few times during the day. She had stopped by the gym a few times to just watch me, and she liked what she saw, so she thought it was only fair that I got to see her. How could any man lie next to that every night and not touch it?

You'd think that this would have led to a face-to-face or face-to-cock meeting, but it didn't. For another few weeks Delia would check me out during her workouts at the gym and then leave me short erotic videos of herself. Sometimes she would be pleasing herself with a vibrator, other times showing off sexy lingerie. Once she was in the shower. She must've been shooting them during the day while no one else was home. It was obvious she enjoyed being my very own soft-core porn star.

When we did talk on the phone I begged to see her. I tried everything. I told her how beautiful she was and how much I wanted her. There was silence on the line. I told her how I could not wait any longer, that I really needed her. I even told her how lonely I was and that she was the only woman for me. All of these lines had worked on women in the past, but they yielded nothing when it came to Delia. Finally one night I asked her, "When exactly do you plan on fucking me?"

She laughed and said, "It's about time you grew a pair and asked for what you wanted. Next weekend would be great because my kids and husband will be up at the lake for their annual fishing trip and Mom gets her annual weekend alone while they rough it." I could not stop grinning. In Delia I had finally met my match.

Friday night could not come fast enough. Delia hadn't been in the gym all week, which only increased my anticipation. I realized that she wasn't going to give me anything until she could give me everything. When the night finally came I found myself standing on the front porch of Delia's home, more nervous than I had been in years, wondering if this was the beginning of something powerful or the beginning of the end. Would this be the one chick I could not shake? The one I would not want to let go of when the time came? I rang the doorbell, and when the door opened, I was again stunned by Delia's beauty. She greeted me warmly and was very proper, being sure to take my coat. I could tell a lot about her just by looking at her home, which was impeccably decorated. Everything was arranged perfectly and tastefully. Even the family photos appeared to have been organized by age, event, and even photo quality, with professional photos up front and candids in the back. Her home was well cared for and much thought had gone into each detail. Delia appeared to be a deliberate woman— there were no accidents in her life.

We sat on the couch in her family room and she offered me a drink. When she returned she kissed me softly on the lips and thanked me for coming. She said she'd had to wait to meet me until she was sure, and now she was. I took Delia's face into my hands and kissed her. She tasted of mint and strawberries and her skin felt cool to the touch. I sensed the hesitancy in her touch, so I broke away from our kiss and leaned Delia back on the sofa. I rolled up her pants legs and removed her heels. Slowly I sucked on each of her toes while massaging her soles and the back of her calves. I ran my hand up the legs of her pants to rub her thighs. Tonight was her night to be teased like she had been doing to me with those videos.

I stood her up and removed her pants and shirt, and when she stood before me in only her panties and bra, I was blown away.

Her body was tight and toned. Hours at the gym and maybe even hours at her surgeon's office had paid off for her. I kneeled before her and kissed her thighs and caressed her butt. I worked my way up to her stomach and she grabbed the back of my head to move my lips to her crotch. I licked and worked the fabric of her panties with my lips. She gasped and moved my head in deeper, but I wanted more. I stood and gently bit her breasts and licked her bra's sheer fabric. Delia grabbed my shirt and tried to get me to take it off, but I wasn't going to give it up so easily. I pushed her down on her knees and flipped her around so that her chest was pressed up against the couch. I fingered her soft red curls and massaged her scalp while kissing her neck. I whispered in her ear what I was going to do to her next and how much she was going to like it. It was then that I took my cock out and started pushing into her through her panties. The fabric was so sheer and smooth it tickled the tip of my penis. I was determined to push my way through.

Delia kept trying to grab her panties and yank them down but I was in her ear saying no, I wanted to work my way into her. Delia may have controlled every aspect of her life, but she was not going to control the way I screwed her. Before I'd made my way in Delia pushed me back and retrieved a condom from the pocket of her pants. I should have known she'd be prepared for everything. Finally I pulled her panties to the side, and right there on the floor of her luxurious family room, with the happy faces of her children and husband staring down on us, I buried myself deep into her. I held Delia tightly and was sure to never let her control the pace or position. I was screwing her the way she needed it. The way her husband probably never did.

Now, there is a gentle balance that has to be struck in order for the sex to be mind-blowing for a married woman. You have to make her feel like a ho, but also make her feel like the one ho in the world that you respect. So before I exploded inside her I pulled out a little, flipped her around, and looked deeply in her eyes. Delia looked back at me like I was a mystery she was trying to crack, probably wondering why was she here with me, why was I being so rough, and why was she enjoying it so much. All women went over these questions in their minds as they tried to understand both their reality and the fantasy now taking place in real time. I leaned in and kissed her lips while I slowly inserted myself into her again. The sex was slow this time and deliberate. I never broke eye contact with her. Delia's skin became flushed and heated as she groped and ground more aggressively. We were going to cum together. Suddenly Delia's body started to shake. She was trying to control it, but the vibrations would not stop. Her body was pulsating and there was very little she could do to mask it. I pushed harder, and I lost control. I came harder than I had in years.

Exhausted, I rested my head on her chest, and I could hear her whispering, "Thank you . . . thank you."

As we lay on her couch that evening she told me how much she hungered for something new in her life. Delia needed to matter, and she felt that meeting me was the first step in getting to know herself again. She'd learned long ago not to be selfish, but the problem with constantly giving is that rarely do others know when to slow up on the take. She'd been empty before tonight, and I'd filled her up. She'd reclaimed more than her sexuality tonight—she'd reclaimed herself.

I listened as she talked. She made us sandwiches and drinks and we watched a late-night movie. We had sex again, this time in the bed she shared with her husband. In the morning I showered and dressed and left her in bed.

On the way home I replayed the night in my head. It was satisfying, but what would come next? Delia would never leave her husband and her comfortable life for me. She was far too smart for that, but I did get the sense that she wanted me to hang around.

She didn't show up at the gym that week, or the next, and she didn't call. I sent her a few emails:

Delia:

Hope all is well with u. I called and left a few messages and you have not called back. I want to c u again.

J

Delia:

I saw u at the gym earlier today and you didn't even look at me. I tried to catch you and you were gone. Did I do something wrong? Did your husband catch on?

Jacob

Delia:

This is getting really weird. Did I do something? I stood across from your house today and watched you play with your kids in the yard. I know you saw me. I was going to come over and speak to you but your husband came out at the same time. Please just call me.

J

And I heard nothing back, until this:

Mr. Morton:

It has been brought to our attention that you have been harassing our client TS432. As you are already aware, TEASE has a "no unwanted communication" policy on our accounts. Once a person has asked for no more contact or has stopped responding, members are asked respectfully to move on to other teasers. Our goal is to keep "Hot Sheet" a safe environment. We have suspended your account for ninety days. If there are no further complaints, we will reinstate your account.

Please note that in your initial agreement we stated that we do reserve the right to reveal your personal information to the local authorities if they approach us as the result of a com-

plaint. No complaint has been filed at this time, but our client has asked us to notify you of her intent if further measures are taken to contact her.

Thanks for your attention to this matter.

Destiny Brooks

Delia's ass was turning me into a stalker. And more than that, without Delia, where am I going to turn to get my next fix?

Xavia

> I am sick of being married but too cowardly to walk away. I love my husband but hate the sex. I spend way too much time wondering about other men's lips, hands, and how they are hung. No one seems to get it—I am looking for the man who can give me more. TS098

I am way too horny for a married woman of forty. Sometimes I scare myself because I simply love men too much and just talking to them isn't enough anymore. I need to know what they feel like, what their fantasies are, and what they would do to me if they had the chance. Don't get me wrong. I am not so horny because I don't get any from my husband. We have sex a few times a week; it's just boring. We stopped kissing years ago and TL has no idea of what sex outside of a bed even is. It has been ten years of married sex that only occurs in bed with absolutely no kissing.

Sometimes it is so bad that I can actually time how long it takes him to cum. The clock is right next to the bed and it usually takes exactly eight minutes. From head to cum, eight minutes—there are no variances, and very rarely do I get a chance to cum or even get a chance to simply do it again. TL is fulfilled. He has sex far more than his boys and I have managed even after three children to still keep myself together. He doesn't seem to expect much sexually from me except to stay shapely and attractive enough for other men to consider me a catch, *his* catch.

The truth is, so many people look at us and wonder how we got it so right. We have been together for fifteen years and married happily for ten. We get along well, are both successful in our careers, and have every toy that you can imagine to prove it. Our three children are smart and well behaved, and we appear to have everything in order. There are not too many women in the world who would not trade places with me.

But though TL is sexy, smart, and caring, he is also a stick-in-the-mud, argumentative, and a lousy lover. It is the hardest thing ever to not be satisfied with someone whom other people want, because there will never be anyone on your side if it all goes wrong. "Xavia is selfish," they will say. No, I am not selfish. I just know that I need more than what I am getting.

Will I ever leave TL? Probably not. Our lives are too intricately linked and our children are great because they have both of us. Things are not horrible on the surface and they are decent enough behind closed doors. It is one of the hardest things to explain. How you can be okay with someone and not be passionate about them? How can you be spouses and not soul mates? How can you love and not be in love anymore? I am all of those things with TL, and I honestly do not know how to make peace with both my desires and the realities of my daily life.

My solution has been simply to cheat. It is the age-old answer for men trapped in marriages that no longer meet all of their needs. I never viewed myself as a cheater. I kind of fell into it, but it's really proven to be my saving grace. Passion with no ties. No one in my circle knows because if they did they would deem me crazy and ungrateful. It is still taboo for a woman to be honest and say that one man cannot meet all of her needs no matter how wonderful he may be. I consider myself a trailblazer, a woman breaking new ground in pursuit of what she wants. I didn't choose this situation, it chose me, and it has been choosing me ever since.

I started sleeping with other men about a year ago during a particularly ugly patch in my marriage. TL was struggling after losing his high-paying finance job due to cutbacks and witnessing the failure of several start-up businesses. I had little time and patience for his latest round of "woe is me." I was so damn busy trying to launch a new product at work there was little room left to think about important things like our kids and the mortgage, let alone TL's midlife crisis. While he was trying to bounce back I was thriving in my new public relations position at a local cosmetics company. I was making money, gaining status, and becoming a talking head for the firm. It seemed that as things got better for me, TL was falling off.

At first it wasn't a huge deal. He'd supported me through the three pregnancies that sidelined me from my work; each time I had to come back fighting for my position and prove that a mom could still be aggressive, creative, and dedicated. Sometimes I was frustrated, but I kept plugging away; not once did I give up. TL started out plugging away, but when the failures started to stack up, he began to just sit around the house and bemoan his situation. When the job opportunities dried up he decided the answer was to start his own thing. I was willing to give him whatever he needed to get something started—$30,000 to make him the king of a dry-cleaning franchise, $13,000 to open a private men's club, $50,000 to start an investment club, all failures for one reason or another. It seemed as if anything he touched was doomed. Nothing was working, so he was just hanging around the house talking about how he needed to work out (never actually doing it), what needed to be fixed around the house (not fixing it), and that the kids needed more to do (but not doing anything with them).

Conventional wisdom said that I should be more patient, that most men go through this life assessment and most do eventually come out ahead. I was prepared for the midlife crisis with the sports car, gold jewelry, and cheating with younger women, but this creature that spent its days and nights on our couch was a mystery to me. It didn't move, was rarely happy, and spent a whole lot of time feeling sorry for itself. I didn't know how to fix it. Luckily, I made more than enough to handle our bills, and the kids were just happy to have Dad home, but I was dying a long, drawn-out emotional death and I had no idea when I would be able to breathe freely again.

One day in the middle of my husband's slow meltdown I received an email at work from Cyrus. The email was a simple one, saying that he had seen a profile of me in a local business magazine and couldn't believe it was me. He wondered if I remembered him, and if I wanted to talk, he'd love to hear from me. When I read the message I knew exactly who he was, and the truth was that I *had* thought of him over the years, wondering if he was married, if he was still in the newspaper industry, and if he ever thought of me. Cyrus and I had met eleven years before, and he was the brother who almost stopped me from marrying my husband.

We worked together at a newspaper, and our on-the-job friendship soon turned into long lunches, relationship talk, and then long conversations at night. We never had more than a lunch date because I was already living with TL and wasn't a cheat; if things started heading in that direction I slowed them down. Once it became apparent to me that I wasn't being fair to Cyrus, I made the hard decision to let him go. By then I had changed jobs and gotten engaged. I had to stop playing with the notion of being just friends with Cyrus when we both knew that we wanted more.

To this day I remember the events that sent me down the path toward marriage. TL was engrossed in some sort of drama with his ex-wife and daughter and told me, as the girlfriend, to let him handle it. No problem usually, but his ex-wife had started harassing me at work, and I was to simply ignore it and let him work it out? Pissed, I called Cyrus and just talked. Not about what was happening between TL and me, but about what I wanted in the future and if I was really ready at such a young age to be married. Cyrus told me to come over. I said no. I knew that if I was with him I would never come back home, and although I was mad, I wasn't sure I wanted to give up everything with TL. Cyrus then suggested that I meet him at a park so we could just talk more. Sounded safe enough, so I met him. That afternoon we laughed and talked about our pasts and what we wanted for the future. It was refreshing to be with someone who had no baggage and who didn't feel he knew everything simply because he was older. Cyrus was the only guy I had been around in years who was close to me in age. Most of the men I'd dated were older—TL by ten years. Back then I fancied myself too sophisticated for men my age; now I know I was just a young girl looking for direction, and I sensed early on that someone my own age couldn't teach me much. That afternoon under the trees, if I had only opened my eyes, I would have seen so clearly that there was a young guy who could meet my needs and that I was moving a little too quickly into the next phase of my life. When Cyrus walked me back to my car he asked me if I wanted to go back to his place just for a while. I said no again. He asked me if I was sure, and I said I was. I was engaged to another man, and in the end, it wasn't worth losing my upcoming marriage over a go-see. He leaned in and kissed me on the lips, and the moment seared itself into my mind. That sliding-door moment when you know that you could be on one of two trains toward different destinies and you choose the one that makes the most sense. I chose a guy who I knew loved me even if he didn't always get me, instead of a guy who liked me but might only want to get in my pants.

That was the last time I saw Cyrus. He called on occasion during the first few years of my marriage to see how I was, and then the calls stopped when I told him I was pregnant with my first child. Maybe that was when he knew that I was really committed to someone else and there was no room for us. Over the years I thought of Cyrus as the one who got away. Had I passed on a life of adventure for the safety and predictability of an established man? Was there more to a relationship than simply being secure? Over time I thought of him less, but I never forgot him.

I emailed him back right away. The email led to our first phone call, which went on for hours. Even after eleven years we got along incredibly well. He was still in the newspaper industry, running circulation for an environmental publication. Oddly enough, he was still single with no kids. There had been a few close calls where he thought he'd found the one, but he'd made peace with the fact that he was indeed too selfish to settle down. Currently he was dancing a delicate waltz between women his age who wanted things from him that he knew he didn't want to give and immature twentysomethings who wanted nothing but whom he was getting far too old and intolerant to chase or play daddy to. Cyrus was successful, funny, open, and kind. TL was none of these things and not doing a damn thing to change it.

We made plans for lunch a week later and in the meantime we talked on the phone as often as we could. I felt as if I was fifteen again and had a forbidden crush. I woke up thinking of him and went to bed with him on my mind. I had a secret no one knew, and it was wonderfully harmless and incredible. The day of our lunch I obsessed over my hair (too long and matronly), my makeup (far too unsophisticated), and my clothes (did I have anything remotely hot anymore?). My mania even extended to my car: did it whisper "sexy woman" or yell "frantic mom" from its grille? Cyrus liked talking to me on the phone, but would he love what he saw? When I knew him all those years ago I was a size 4, with lush long hair and an innocent spirit. Three kids, one marriage, and a hectic career later, I'd become a seductive size 10, with sensible hair and a jaded perspective on life and its potential to please.

Cyrus and I met at a small restaurant near his job. I arrived first, so nervous. For just a lunch with an old friend, the stress level was incredible. When he walked in I recognized him immediately. Not much had changed over the years; he was still beautiful and incredibly sexy—tall and thin and the color of fine chocolate. He smiled and his dimples were still there, along with his luscious lips. He sat down and we drifted into an easy conversation. We were both definitely more mature, but our attraction was still incredibly strong. At one point we were so relaxed with each other that when I rested my hand on the table Cyrus covered it with his. He held my hand like that for some time, and I tried to ignore the heat tingling up my arm. It felt warm, inviting, and comforting. Just that small touch made me feel safe and cared for—something that had been missing from my life for some time.

When I remembered that I needed to get back across town to pick up my youngest son from day care, Cyrus thanked me for coming out and offered to walk me back to my car. Once at my car I thanked him for lunch and leaned in to hug him goodbye. When I pulled away he kissed me on the forehead, which has always been my weakness, the one thing that will endear any man to me. I closed my eyes and in those short few seconds I caught a small glimpse of all that I was missing with my husband and everything I could have right now. This moment in this parking garage was safe and I wanted it more than anything else in the world. Cyrus worked his lips from my forehead to my right cheek and then to my lips. He kissed me, and all my years of not being kissed melted away. His taste was sublime and this experience freeing, euphoric. I hadn't felt like this in years and didn't want this moment to stop. In his kiss was desire and need aimed at me.

I pulled away first, slightly paranoid from mental images of one of my husband's friends driving by and seeing me making out in a parking lot. Honestly, I didn't care, but I also knew this kiss was more than I could handle and that it was best that I break away before I combusted. How could a kiss be this good? Why didn't I feel guilty? Why did I want it to go further? He opened my door for me, and I got into the car. He leaned in and gave me a quick kiss and said that he'd enjoyed lunch, and then he was off back to work. I watched him walk away and wondered if I'd made a mistake eleven years before? Here he was, so successful, beautiful, and delicious all these years later, and our pull was stronger than ever. Was Cyrus the man I should have been with?

When I finally got myself together enough to drive and had just pulled out of the garage, my cell phone rang. It was Cyrus. We laughed about how nervous we both had been during lunch and how strange it was to still be so connected all these years later. We talked all the way to the day care center, and even after hanging up I could still feel the heat of his body on my skin and softness of his lips on mine. That evening all through dinner all I could think about was Cyrus. I was happy and excited, two things that rarely occurred in my daily routine. Later that night once the boys were asleep and TL was knocked out on the couch, I went upstairs to my office and emailed him:

C:
I know that it is incredibly late, but I just wanted to thank you again for lunch. I have not laughed so much in a very long time. All evening long I thought of you and little else—and even if this was the last time, I just wanted to let you know that it was great being with you today. Thanks for coming back.
Xavia

I was about to log off when my email notifier chimed with a message. It was from Cyrus.

X:
It was great seeing you too. What are you doing up so late? I know if I was with you, you would not be sending emails at 1:00 a.m. We'd be getting it in :)—just joking. You are still one of the coolest chicks ever and hopefully we will get to do it again. Hopefully I did not ruin your evening, but that does not mean to stop thinking about me because I have definitely been thinking about you.
C

It was just an email, yet it warmed me. He wanted me. Thought I was interesting, even. This was just a harmless flirtation. Just like the guys at work or some of my clients, right? No, this was not like that at all because I wanted to ride this flirtation out. This was not a coy smile, a flash of cleavage, or a pat on the arm. This was a kiss that had made me wet and excited and I wanted more. And for the first time in a long time I was going to step out and get what I needed.

• • •

Cyrus and I talked all week, mainly during the day while we were at work or late at night when my house was quiet and he was riding home from his latest disastrous date. We talked a lot about how we'd arrived at the major decisions in our lives. I shared with him how the early years of my marriage were a dream until routine and disappointments started to wear us down. Cyrus talked about how he had met many wonderful sisters but that none of them in the end were really worth changing his game plan for. We were both people simply stuck in situations of our own making, trying to find a little fun in the muck.

The flirting did not stop, of course. Cyrus did not hide the fact that he wanted to see me again as soon as possible. He knew that I wanted to be with him, he would say, and obviously I needed more than what I was getting to be so drawn to him. How right he was. It was so bad that when TL and I had sex, I imagined they were Cyrus's hands and lips and could almost hear Cyrus whispering scintillating words to me, like "I am the best that you'll ever have," and "Do you want more?"

One night TL went out to another get-rich-quick sales meeting and Cyrus happened to call. He told me that he had to be blunt with me, that the whole phone thing was not working for him, and he wanted to see me again; he thought of me to the point of distraction. He actually had a date planned for that night but wanted to check to see if I wanted to get together instead.

I gave him the same hollow words that I had been giving him

for two weeks: we could only be friends, I didn't cheat, and he really didn't want to do this; he was just enjoying the challenge of me being out of reach.

Cyrus said he was a grown man and knew what he wanted. "Don't worry about me," he said. "It's about what you want to do."

I was conflicted at first. A good wife and mother does not cheat on her family or need more than what her husband is able to give her. What the hell was wrong with me? Then I thought about all the hard work, dedication, and support that I'd poured over TL and his situations, and thought, *Why the hell not?* I deserved passion and the attention of a man all about me, if only for a few hours. An evening with Cyrus was far more intriguing than another night of home improvement shows on HGTV and a bottle of wine. TL would be out late attending his meeting and then hanging out with his boys. I knew I could easily call a sitter, go see Cyrus, and get back home without TL knowing I'd ever stepped out of the house. It was time to feed my needs, and the place to start was with Cyrus.

I pulled up in front of Cyrus's house and sat in the driveway for a few minutes. Once the decision had been made to go, the logistics were quick to work out. I'd called Brittany to sit for a few hours and told the boys that I had to go to the office to pull together a press release. The part that had taken the longest was showering, choosing an outfit, and figuring out what the hell to do with my hair. Like a lot of women who have been married awhile, I'd developed a uniform of looking okay, a veil of passable beauty that didn't call too much attention to myself (to not make other moms nervous) yet was sexy enough to keep my husband mildly interested (holding on to the long hair I hated). Luckily, after three boys my body was still pretty tight, and I looked good in my clothes, but now, standing in front of the mirror, I saw the stretch marks from the pregnancies, the soft belly, and the slight decent of my boobs, like they were just exhausted from being. My clothes were all safe, mostly tracksuits and sensible business suits—nothing sexy for a night out. After ten minutes of back-and-forth and self-pity, I opted for my best-fitting jeans and a bra-strap tank. Underneath I had on my only sexy underwear set, a black lace affair that I'd bought on a whim at a friend's lingerie party six months earlier hoping that one day TL and I would be in the mood at the same time and I could whip this out. I added a sexy pair of heels, but my hair was hopeless, just long and straight. I was lucky to get my touch-up every six weeks; who had time to figure out some youthful and sexy style? So as I did most days, I pulled it back into a bun.

In the end I looked at myself with both disbelief and wonder. Was I really going to meet a man at his house, and what would I do once I got there? The odds were that I would panic and just leave, but what if I did not leave and gave in to where I dreamed the night would take me?

After I rang the bell, Cyrus came to the door, and as always, I was amazed at how beautiful he was, the deep cocoa shade of his skin and the jet black hair of his goatee magnificently outlining his lips. He hugged me, thanked me for coming over, and asked me if I wanted something to drink. I said no, as I was still feeling like I might bolt at any minute, and having a drink in hand might slow me up. His home was typical for a brother who lives alone but likes nice things—all the rooms decorated like a showroom in a high-end furniture store, with an obvious lack of the warmth that comes from having a woman and a family in the house. Cyrus's place was about knocking a woman out and allowing her to feel that there was space for her in his world.

I love little man tricks!

As he took me from room to room and told me about the great deal he'd gotten on the house, I started to relax. I no longer felt like this was my first booty call in years, but that I was just visiting an old friend. We finally made our way to his family room and I sat down on the couch. *See, this isn't bad, Xavia,* I thought. *You can handle this.* That was until Cyrus sat down next to me.

Cyrus looked at me and said, "Nothing is going to happen here that you don't want. I want—I *need* you to be comfortable." Then he asked me, "What did you want to do?"

This moment—an easy, intimate situation with someone I was attracted to—might never happen again. I could do the right thing, admit that this was bad, and leave, or I could be honest and do what I desired: stay and be with this man. So much of my life was about doing what was right—what was expected. This night was going to be about giving Xavia what she wanted. Cyrus began to look uneasy while all of these thoughts fought for position in my head. He looked at me one final time with sort of a "what is it going to be" look, and I made the decision. On his couch on that Saturday night it started, and I have not been the same since.

I leaned in and kissed Cyrus. It was as good as it was that afternoon in the garage. In his kiss was longing, desire, and anticipation. This was not going to be some routine dance—this was special. Every inch of me just wanted to feel his weight on me. To be engulfed by all of him. He leaned into me and pushed me back on his couch. I wrapped my legs around him tightly and he whispered in my ear that he'd waited so long for this. Suddenly he broke our kiss and sat up, pulling me along with him. He turned on the lamp next to the couch and slowly began to remove his clothes. The skin on his tall, lean body was incredibly smooth. His shoulders were wide, his waist tiny, and his ass amazingly round. My eyes loved dancing all over his body because it was so different from what I was used to. TL was short, hairy, and thick-waisted. He was far more attractive with his clothes on.

With every item of clothing he took off he was sure to kiss each newly exposed part of me. Off came the bra, my shoes, and the jeans. As he kissed my breasts, belly, calves, and feet, I could not wait for him to get to my panties. While he toured my body with his mouth my eyes took in his dick, fully erect and wanting. Cyrus would not let me touch him. He wanted to touch me. He was kissing my lower belly and inching closer and closer toward my core, and I wanted him to just take the panties off. It had been so long since a man had undressed me. Even on my honeymoon night TL had fallen asleep on the bed while I was taking my shower; he'd apologized but said that I took too long in the bathroom and he could not help it. That night and every night since I have undressed myself in bed. But this night brought that streak to a throbbingly delicious end.

Suddenly Cyrus pulled away. He told me to let my hair down. My long relaxed mop was interesting to him? I unpinned my bun, and my tresses spilled over my shoulders. Cyrus got up from the couch and sat down on the floor. He just looked at me intently and I got a little nervous. What did he see? Why was he so fascinated? Was he ever going to take off my panties? I had to ask him if anything was wrong. "No," he said. "I just wanted to see you again." And with that he kneeled in front of me on the couch and placed one of my legs on each of his shoulders. He grabbed my butt and scooted me closer to him. With one of the most fluid moves ever he pulled my panties off and threw them aside. Placing one hand on my belly and with the other grabbing my butt, Cyrus began to lick me deep inside. The warmth of his tongue along with the sounds that he made were making me even wetter. When he moved up to my clit and alternated between licking and blowing on it I thought I would lose my mind. Every once in a while he would give me a gentle bite on my pussy lips and tell me how I tasted and how he could not get enough. Cyrus wanted to know how things felt and what I was thinking. He was oral in more ways than just one.

He pulled me to the floor and lay on top of me. He kissed me, putting his tongue deep inside my mouth, and his dick finally made its presence known. Cyrus was smaller than TL, but far more adept at using it. I had never had an orgasm from intercourse alone and within minutes I could barely stand the tingling sensations as Cyrus's dick hit me in all the right places. I had heard that there was a G-spot, but this brother had G-spot GPS. His dick was doing things to me that I had not thought were possible, and I could not get enough. Cyrus buried his face in my neck, telling me that if he were my man, he'd be in this every day. Damn. This talking stuff I could get used to.

Right when I started to feel my legs shake, Cyrus pulled out. He turned me onto my knees and was going to get at it from behind. Before entering me he slowly rubbed my shoulders and asked me if I was okay. I told him I was fine and not to stop. He kissed me down my back and kissed and licked my hips and butt. Slowly he began to kiss each butt cheek and then he stuck his tongue in my ass. I pulled away a little; no one had ever done that to me. The sensations were so strong. It felt incredible. I began moving with the rhythm of his tongue

He would lick my ass and then my pussy, and the sensations were making me light-headed. Then he entered me from behind and my pussy locked around him. Cyrus loved to go deep and slow. He wanted to please me and get his at the same time. While he was fucking me he kept saying, "Damn, Xavia, do you know how long I've wanted to be with you?" That was true for me as well, but I was consumed with my sensations and breathless from the sex—there was little energy left to speak.

• • •

Cyrus pulled out and rolled over onto his back. I lay on top of him kissing his chest and waist before burying my nose into the blackness that was the hair around his dick. He smelled of me and him and the mixture was mind-blowing. I wanted to taste him, lick him, but before I could he pulled me up face-to-face with him, telling me, "There will be plenty of time for that later." With that he sat me on top of him and told me to look him in the face. Cyrus dug his fingers into my hips and I pushed him even deeper inside me. At one point I forgot where I was and I was concerned only with the pulsing of my pussy and his breath, which he was having a hard time controlling underneath me. Cyrus was ready to cum and I knew it. He pulled me down to him belly to belly and held me tight. He pumped harder and harder into me while holding me by my hair. Once he was there he let out that guttural noise universal for all men when they are pleased. Years ago I had a friend tell me that the cum was universal, but what really mattered was what he did after. If you're just a booty call, he will kiss you or say something sweet and move away: go to the bathroom, shift to the other side of the bed, go get a drink—a move to place distance between himself and the situation. If he cares, he will hold you, talk to you, play with you—he wants to feel connected and he wants you to know that it was more than just a hit. This was the test.

Cyrus rolled me over onto my back, leaned over me, and said one thing: "Do you regret your decision years ago?"

I thought about my wedding, my boys, and the good times and drama with TL. I was honest with Cyrus and said, "No, but I really don't regret my decision today."

Cyrus wrapped his arms around me from behind and we lay there on the floor in front of his fireplace. I had no idea what he was thinking, but I know what was on my mind. I was satisfied and excited about what was to come and scared that I would never be happy at home again.

Cyrus and I met regularly for months afterward, always on a Friday night, when TL was too preoccupied with one wacked business scheme or another to notice my absence. The boys were actually happy to have so many play dates where they didn't have to go home early and get ready for school the next day. And of course, my pussy and I had never been more satisfied. But with each orgasm, each time I called out Cyrus's name, and each tightening of my lips around his dick, he felt the connection growing stronger. Afterward, he was always begging me to stay, and started to grow resentful that my answer was always the same: "I have to go home."

And it was true. My looks were changing. I traded in my tracksuits for formfitting jeans and shirts that, though sensible enough for a mother to cavort in with her boys, weren't so rough on the eyes. I spent an extra hour in the salon getting my hair cut into layers that preserved the length—which *both* men in my life found irresistible—while adding a bit of pizzazz that I could easily manage every day. To this day, I think TL noticed what was happening inside me—whether or not he knew there was someone else, or was just afraid there *could be* one day, I'll never know—and started to more aggressively pursue new job leads. He was back in his expensive suits, out of the house early for interviews, and coming home too late and too tired to have a pity party.

One Friday afternoon before TL left to meet his boys, he caught me half dressed in the kitchen, wearing a bathrobe and a new lace thong, preparing to see Cyrus. He said, "Hold up for a second, I have something to tell you," and went on to tell me that he was "back in the game," that he'd landed a job as a VP of finance at a Fortune 500 firm recently moved to the area to take advantage of all Baltimore was offering to stimulate business development. Totally unexpectedly, TL pushed my panties aside and made love to me right on the countertop, thanking me with each thrust for being his supporter, his lover, his encourager. And although I was incredibly wet—that was more passion than we'd shared in years—it still only took eight minutes.

When TL zipped up his pants and headed off to share the good news with his boys, I understood—I didn't need to be loved more, I just needed to be fucked harder. And just as I'd tried to avoid doing all those years ago, I had been stringing Cyrus along. I had it all: a man who satisfied me inside my panties and made me feel sexy and desirable, and a man who I knew couldn't live without me, despite his lackluster ways of showing it. That night when I went to see Cyrus, I apologized. It wasn't fair of me to demand of him what I did and to offer nothing but good sex in return.

Cyrus said he got it; he'd figured TL would step up to the plate at some point, and just begged me to be sure I wasn't making the same mistake again. "You know we'll probably never have this chance again once you walk out that door." I walked up to him and put my arms around him, to give him one final kiss, which turned into one final palming of my ass, which was then one final finger into my pussy, and then one final round in front of the fireplace, clothes half on, half off, Cyrus forcefully thrusting his dick into me, as if to punish me for leaving while simultaneously begging me to stay. "No . . . one . . . is . . . ever . . . going . . . to . . . fuck . . . you . . . this . . . deep . . . this . . . hard . . . this . . . lovely . . . ever . . . again," he said, right before I screamed his name one final time. I felt tears fall down my cheeks when I came, and they didn't stop until I was within sight of my home.

Since then, TL's been happy; he was almost instantly promoted at work and is back on top, in fact even higher than his previous peak. There's a bit more variety in our lovemaking, but nothing that will sustain me the way Cyrus did. So I now scour the pages of *TEASE*, looking for an occasional tryst with someone who will understand that I'm not available for anything more than a few hours of mind-blowing, pussy-numbing sex, and who won't have me distracted from my daily life with imaginings of what could be. Thank you, Cyrus, for showing me what I need, and thank you, *TEASE*, for helping me find it whenever the urge comes calling.

Destiny

Gotta Love Donuts

Pet play is my thing. Not into doing it with my dog, just enjoy having pets watch. Want to meet an animal lover who doesn't mind doing it truly doggy style. TS781

t is another weekend and I'm at home alone with no date. Josh keeps calling, but I can't stand him, and Denae, whom I would love to spend time with, will not call me back—it's the story of my life.

I met Josh about four months ago at a CD launch event. He was cute—not knock-you-out fine, but intelligent and available—so that night, in a sea of thugs, posers, and stylists, he was my best bet. The drinks were flowing from the open bar and the scene at the club was otherworldly. The venue was designed to look like a forest, and there were little birds flying from tree to tree inside the club while women covered in platinum body paint served finger

foods. Josh and I got liquored up fast, and he was being so atten-
tive and wonderful that at three o'clock, when he asked me if I
wanted to go back to his place, I said yes.

We walked two blocks to his apartment, a beautiful studio
overlooking the harbor. Josh started to kiss me, and it had been a
while since I had last had sex, so a sister was taking off her
clothes, taking off his clothes, unwrapping a condom, and singing
a resounding chorus of "Oh shit" within minutes of walking in
the door. Josh had a small dick and average fucking skills. From
the way that he just lay there when I was riding him to the silly-ass
grin on his face, I knew that this type of stuff did not happen to
him often. However, as much as I wanted to just get mine and
leave, I'm not a bitch, so I let him wrap his arms around me, I
placed my head on his chest, and we just looked out of his windows at the water until we both fell asleep.

The next morning I awoke to the sound of paper bags being
opened and smooth jazz playing softly in the studio. I looked over
and saw Josh, dressed in sweats, placing donuts on a tray and
making coffee in the kitchen. I sat up in bed looking for my
clothes, and Josh told me that he had gotten us breakfast and that
I could go grab a quick shower. I wanted to leave. In the light of
day it was even more apparent that Josh and I maybe should not
have hooked up. I did not know him, and he was going to force
me to play the morning-after game, where one of us tries to convince the other that we will see each other again. I knew it was not
going to happen. I saw that he had laid my things out neatly on a
chair near the bed, and I grabbed them and went into the bathroom. There on the counter was a towel, an unopened toothbrush,
designer soap, and a small flower. How sweet. I was starting to
really feel like an ass for not appreciating this brother's efforts.

Once I emerged from the bathroom, Josh invited me to sit
down and have breakfast. He wanted to get to know me, and I
wanted to get out of there. "What do you do?" he asked.

"I write."

"What do you write?"

"I work at a newspaper."

I never asked what he did or complimented him on his great place. Josh tried asking me about my interests, what I was going to do with the rest of my day, and so on and so on, but I wouldn't bite. He was a good guy, but not the guy for me. He was laying it all out there for me in a neat package, and perfect men scare me. Give me a grungy, difficult guy any day because his dirt is there for all to see. Mr. Nice Josh was obviously Mr. Smart Josh too, because eventually he gave up, cleared the dishes, and told me that I could let myself out because he was going to take a shower. I felt bad for not playing along, but I knew that any signs of interest would attach him to me forever . . . or at least until he asked me to shit on his foot.

About a week later I was at work when Deanna called me up front. There on her desk was a small bouquet of flowers of the same variety as the one that Josh had left for me in his bathroom. Deanna could not contain her excitement, so I let her read the card. It was from Josh, of course, thanking me for a wonderful evening and apologizing if he'd come on too strong. He wanted to see me again and included his number.

Deanna was all over herself with praise for Josh's thoughtfulness. I even had to admit that the flowers were beautiful, and I went back to my desk to call Josh and say a quick thanks. I started out pretty succinct with a thank-you and asking how he'd found out where I work. He mentioned that I'd happened to have on a *TEASE* shirt (love the stylish office freebies) that night and he thought that would be a great place to start. Turns out Josh was a social worker and a transplant from New York. His cousin was the artist whose CD was being launched the other night. Josh said that I should call him if I wanted to hang out. I have been dodging his calls ever since because I broke my rule and gave him a way in.

• • •

While I am not at all into the nice guys, it's open season on the dysfunctional! Denae is a local promoter who places artist and club ads in the paper all the time. Everything about him—from his looks (dead-on tall and sexy from head to toe—I know, I checked out his toes) to his swagger (his fleet of luxury cars and condo downtown) and his words (all of the ladies in the office are "baby")—says, *Destiny, run away from this brother,* but his game is top-shelf. Denae knows women want him and he knows how to play them. I saw him coming and stayed out of the fray until he walked into my office one day, sat down, and crossed his legs, and his size 11 feet popped up in my view. He removed his jacket and the chocolate thickness of his arms made me forget my own damn name when he asked. He wanted to stop by and invite me to a new venue he was promoting, and he gave me a VIP invite. When he left my office and I got myself together, I asked the others in the office if they'd been invited. Nope, I was the only one.

The club scene is torture for me. The only time I go is when I'm on assignment for the paper. That night I was hoping to see Denae, blow his mind real quick with a hot outfit and a little flirting, and go home. When I arrived, he was nowhere in sight. I shared an uncomfortable VIP couch with two women who obviously had spent more on their hair and makeup than I did on my mortgage. Guys were buzzing around them like bees and I was sitting there trying to hold my own with some berry lip gloss and my "I go to the hairdresser tomorrow" pullback. One of the girls was going on and on about how her man is an asshole and she doesn't know why she came tonight, because the crowd was lame. She cut her eyes at me and then took a sip of her drink. I decided that no man was worth the quick plummeting of my self-esteem and made my way from the VIP area down to the main exit, where I saw Denae standing at the door. "You leaving already?" he said.

"Yeah, it's not really my scene. But I was hoping to see you and say thanks for the invite. I will give it a real good write-up in the paper next week." Denae shook his head and took my arm and led me outside.

"It's a little loud in there. Destiny, I did not invite you for a write-up," he said. "I already have that covered. I just thought you'd have a good time and maybe I could steal a dance. I've seen you a few times at the office and wanted to say something, and Thursday was my chance." I hardly heard what he was saying because I was staring at the smoothness of his lips. The warmth of his hand on my arm was making me want to get closer. I would have done anything for Denae in that moment. He was sexy as hell and I wanted a taste.

We went on one date after that night. Denae did not call and ask me out. He just showed up at the office about two weeks after the club night, said there was a break in his schedule, and asked if I wanted to go out to eat with him later. Everything inside said that I should say no and that a man with "a break in his schedule" had not been thinking of me endlessly over the last few weeks, but I wanted to experience Denae and make sure that he was an ass before I turned him away. The combination of his butt in those jeans, his cologne, the leather seats in his Mercedes, the way he licked his lips when he spoke, and the way his knees constantly brushed mine under the table all made me think that I might be the one for him, the one who would tame the player. All of his game was working on me. Plus, I loved the way he seemed to know everyone, from the guy who parked the car, to the owner of the restaurant and the hostesses (player alert!). I had a taste of being his lady. When he kissed me on my porch and pushed his way into my house, telling me that I wanted it and that I needed it, I was momentarily brain-dead and let him come in.

Denae revealed a body chiseled beyond perfection. He leaned over me, stroking himself (he was huge—shoes never lie) and telling me that I'd never forget this—and he was right. He positioned me perfectly each time and called me baby, at first softly and then louder as his hardness melted inside me. Denae was a pleasure pro and extremely skilled. I had orgasm after orgasm and then he massaged my head until I went to sleep. In the morning he was gone. The next night he sent me a text message saying he had an early meeting and that last night was "ridiculous." That was a month ago and all I get from Denae are texts. He never calls, comes by, or asks me out, and he sure as hell doesn't send flowers.

Tonight I am alone, dodging a good guy's call and praying for the calls of a bad brother. What is wrong with me? Why can't I be about guys who are all about me? Maybe because nice guys don't whisper in your ear that they are going "to fuck you hard until you lose your mind." And right now I prefer a great fuck over a tray of donuts.

Cassandra

Legs of a stallion and the spirit to match. I love taking my pooch for walks. Looking for fellas willing to take a nightly walk with me in the park. I will leave myself open and you can come inside. TS010

don't even know when this started. Who am I kidding? I know exactly when. It was two years ago—four years into my marriage to Dave. I was with a man who adored me and we were on the path of marital and familial bliss. I thought things were perfect and was planning to keep them that way. I did not want a repeat of either my parents' stale marriage or that of Dave's parents, who only stayed together for their children and split when their kids were grown and out of the house. Our marriage was going to be the real deal.

So it was important for me to keep Dave sexually captivated. I was determined to be his fantasy girl and did whatever it took to keep him excited and up! From pouring champagne on his balls on our wedding night to having him eat me in his childhood bedroom while visiting his parents on vacation, whatever Dave wanted sexually he got, with one exception.

One night he came to me with the idea of going to a sex club. Group sex was a longtime fantasy of his and probably the one thing that I could never really wrap my brain around. In my mind, group sex meant going to a person's house and being surrounded by fat old couples looking to score with the only young couple in the room—all the smells and cellulite were not going to be a turn-on. One-on-one was cool, but one with forty? Too much.

• • •

After a few months of giving him everything else he wanted outside of the group scenario, Dave came up with the idea of walking the dog. He'd found it on one of his porn sites—we are pro-computer-porn in our house—and wanted to know if I'd be interested in trying it out. The concept was simple: you go to a lover's lane or park and leave your car doors open. You make out with your partner and whoever stops by to watch is free to jump in as well. You could even send out an email notice or visit a "walking the dog" Web site to let people know where you were going to be.

Dave was quick to point out that it was one-on-one sex with strangers and an opportunity for him to watch me with others. For him it was going to be like the hottest porn ever because he knew the star and could actually fuck her when it was done. I agreed to go through with it because it was spontaneous and random and gave me a chance to perform before an audience. There is nothing sexier than knowing someone is getting off watching you get it on!

After much research, we set our initial walking date and location. We noticed that a local park was already on the national site's list, and we were hoping that if we did everything right things would jump off.

Saturday night Dave and I carefully dressed for our evening. I loved to watch his tanned chest glisten as he put on his lotion. He was truly a beautiful man, with jet black hair and green eyes that I'd loved from day one. He wasn't tall, but I learned long ago that shorter men oftentimes had tighter bodies, and Dave was striking from head to toe and looked as good with his clothes on as he did with them off. He had the body of a man who did physical work daily. The subtle tan that he picked up during the week as a landscaper made him look exotic and dark. Dave did not have a Bally's body; he had more of an old-school, "I work for my money" body. I was getting wet just looking at him.

I was not sure what to wear. Should I be naked under a trench coat? Something crotchless, maybe? What exactly is proper attire when you are going to be fucking strangers at midnight in your local park in the backseat of your Chevy Aveo? Sensing my apprehension, Dave walked over to the closet and pulled out a chocolate tank dress, noting that it would provide easy access while showcasing my 36Ds and twenty-three-inch waist. The chocolate color was always my favorite because with my long curly black hair and mocha complexion, it made my skin look rich. I strapped on my gold heels, and we made our way to the car and off to the park.

When we pulled up there was little to no traffic in the park. We'd expected more people. There were a few gay cruisers and a drunken teen couple on a park bench uncomfortably trying to get it on; experienced freaks know this cannot be done. We sat bored for a few moments more. Dave wondered why no one responded to the typical walking signs: interior lights on in the car, headlights on, door open, and music playing. My man wasn't getting his walk-by stranger sex, but I decided that we could still make the night hot. We might not be walking the dog, but we could definitely play with my pooch.

I leaned the seat back on the passenger side of the car, raised the bottom of my dress up over my hips, and licked my fingers. I removed my moist fingers from my mouth and placed them over my clit. I slowly rocked my fingers back and forth as the scent of my body started to fill the air. Dave always loved the way I smelled and sounded, and when he heard my soft moaning he turned to me and saw me warming myself up for the main event. He watched me for some time as I switched up caressing my clit and finger-fucking myself. I saw him rubbing himself through his jeans as he watched.

I knew that Dave's first instinct would not be to jump in immediately. I always found overeagerness annoying in a man—like he thought that sex was not sex until he was in it. Dave knew that I could get the party started and finished all alone, and he loved to watch. I pulled the top of my dress down and cupped both of my breasts, slowly licking my left nipple. Dave loved my brown nipples because he thought they were big and beautiful and a far cry from the little pink ones he was used to exploring. As my tongue made its way around my nipples I saw that Dave was more aggressively rubbing himself. He wanted release, but he wanted me to get mine first, which that night meant I had to keep teasing him. "Sweetie, you can feel these up, but you cannot kiss them and you have to keep your dick in your pants," I said to Dave as I moved closer for him to pinch and stroke them. It was shaping up to be a hot night after all.

I went back to finger-fucking myself, and when I was on the edge of exploding I removed his hands from my breasts and pushed his arms back over his head. I undid his zipper and pulled his dick out. It was beautifully smooth, and while not the longest dick I have ever had, it was the thickest, and it massaged places inside of me that previous lovers had never even known existed. I licked my left hand and began to slowly rub him up and down. With my right hand I continued to tickle my clit. I was getting ready to cum and nothing was going to stop it. In my ear I could hear Dave begging me for one lick, a tug, or to massage his balls. *Not tonight, dear,* I thought. Tonight it was all about the manual release, and his was quick and hearty. His breathing quickened and he yelled my name and that I shouldn't stop. Hearing his voice and seeing his pleasure all over the front of his jeans gave me permission to cum. My body twisted under the heat and my mind went blank as my vagina grew even wetter. I thought to myself, *Forget walking the dog. Tonight you walked your man's dick,* and that was as good a night as any.

I pulled my dress back down over my thighs and leaned to lick Dave's sweetness from the front of his jeans. I liked the way he tasted and I made sure to feast on him. After licking him clean I came up and kissed his lips and realized that all I needed was in the car that night. As I leaned over to finish fixing my clothes I noticed that there was a young man watching us. He slowly approached the car with his zipper open. He stood by my passenger door. He reached into his trousers and pulled his dick out. It was grand in every way. Truly a sight to see. He rubbed it, and I looked over to Dave trying to decide if this was really happening. He simply leaned back into the door and nodded as if to say, *This is what we wanted.* I wanted Dave to start the car and pull off or to tell the man to leave, but a part of me found it thrilling to have a new dick in my face and my husband giving me permission to play with it. I kissed the head and while he stroked his dick from base to tip my lips and tongue provided just enough moisture to make his brown skin shimmer in the darkness. I wanted to get fucked by this artful strange cock, so I pushed Mr. Strange Dick back and got out of the car. I caught a quick glimpse of his face. He wasn't fine, not ugly, not tall, not short—average in every way except for his tremendous cock, which I think was about eleven inches, and when our eyes met I knew that I wanted every inch of him in me.

He flipped me around and hiked up my dress, exposing my butt, which he slowly massaged. He didn't put his dick inside me but simply rubbed it in between my butt cheeks while pushing them tightly together. It was strangely erotic. I don't have a big butt, but he was able to get enough of me to surround his cock and get him off. This rubbing went on for a few minutes and all along my face was in the car and I was fighting to try to neutralize the pleasure of Mr. Strange Dick's rubbing and still be connected to Dave. Dave just watched my face as I got flushed and my eyes began to close. Oddly, Mr. Strange Dick was not hitting any of my pleasure points but he was pleasing me still. He told me to push back, and he grabbed me more roughly from behind. This made me give out a small scream, and Dave reached out to rub my shoulders and breasts. His wife was cheek-fucking a strange man in the park, and Dave could not wait to get home and do the same thing. Mr. Strange Dick started rocking back and forth and then suddenly I felt him let go and fall to the ground. I heard him moan and then run off into the dark with his open belt buckle clanking. As I stood outside the car trying to adjust my clothes I caught a glimpse of Dave's smile and wondered who was turned on more. Was it Mr. Strange Dick, aroused by the opportunity to fuck a lady in front of her husband, or was it my husband, finally fueling his naughtiest fantasy? Too much thought for such a pleasure-filled night. We pulled out of the park and went home.

Since that night we've walked the dog about every three months—and we've added cheek-fucking to our regular sexual repertoire. The idea of fucking strangers is intoxicating for us, and I guess on some level it allows us to recapture the excitement of our first time together. We have had a few great experiences and some options we thought it best to turn down. And placing personal ads in "Hot Sheet" has yielded the best results. We're creating our own network of dog walkers. Just think what other discoveries are out there.

Celin

saw this ad and lost my mind! Just what I've been looking for: a lady who loves to be ambushed. My dick gets hard at the scent of a woman's terror, her slight resistance, and her eventual surrender. Don't get it twisted: I am not a predator or rapist. I don't force a woman to do anything that she has not agreed to beforehand. My attacks are welcomed by my Vickys (victims)—it's all part of our sex play. Vickys just never know when they'll see me and with what degree of force. Strange? Don't be so quick to judge.

For me attack sex really jumped off with Alecia. I met Alecia at my line brother Tug's place about a year ago. It was one of those sorry-ass "parties" that singles throw right before the holidays *hoping* to find Mr./Ms. Right and not have to spend another holiday season feeling lonely. No one in the room intrigued me. There was the typical mix of high-achieving, "I don't need a man but I really do" sisters, the "if you only tell me that I'm hot when I'm obviously not and I'll do anything for you" loser sisters, and then the total package sisters with great brains, body, and attitude that you could only get to if you fought your way to the top of the hungry man mountain surrounding them. That night, I was not in the mood for scraps or macking my way to the top of that mountain. So I was just chilling listening to the music, taking in the sights, and sipping my drink. And then I noticed Alecia. She wasn't part of any of the cliques in the room. She was friendly with everyone but clearly comfortable just observing. She noticed that I was staring at her and waved me over to join her on the couch.

"See, if you are real quiet you will notice my girl Brianna is quite drunk and buying all of Tug's bullshit right about now," said Alecia.

"Naw, looks to me like your girl is under my man Tug's spell. She wants to walk away but is drawn in by the power of the Unforgiven that my man bathed in before coming downstairs," I responded.

Alecia giggled and said, "Wow, that's what Diddy smells like? No wonder my girl can't resist." We both tried to muffle our laughter at the thought. Tug had been my boy since college and had been chasing Brianna, who was a member of our sister sorority, since 2002, though she'd cut him down at every turn. But Brianna had just been through a pretty public breakup with a local councilman, and after a few drinks she was on Tug's lap telling him every dirty detail of the split. Rebound pussy is better than no pussy, and my boy was rounding the bases with record speed.

"I am Alecia, by the way." Alecia extended her hand to me, and I could not help noticing how small she was; my hand swallowed hers whole.

"I'm Celin. Are you as bored as I am?"

"Sort of, yes and no. Watching others crash and burn getting their mack on never grows old. It gives me new material. I'm a writer, so the interpersonal stuff is always fascinating, but I'm really just here for my girl. The guys in Baltimore have not yet warmed to my Cali flavor."

Alecia leaned in again and said, "If I were a good friend, I would go get her and take her home, but honestly, I think she needs his nice ass to get over the jackass, so I am just going to sit here and sip my drink."

"My boy has wanted that woman for the last six years. I would personally have to take you down if you stepped into that love circle right there." Both Alecia and I looked over at Tug trying his hardest and Brianna too drunk to say no, and Alecia threw both her arms in the air in surrender. I liked her—she was fun.

"In that case, Celin, get me a drink so that maybe I can meet my Mr. Right too."

Alecia was a natural beauty. There was no hint of makeup, and her curly hair was pulled back into a huge puffy ponytail at the base of her neck. She was the color of a coconut shell, and she smelled of berries. Her whole vibe said that she had no one to impress but her damn self. It turned out that she and Brianna were sorors and that she had just moved back to Baltimore after living in L.A. for a few years. She was a pretty successful sitcom writer out there but had grown tired of the scene.

"In L.A. everyone is beautiful and fabulous. I was hungry for flaws, so I came back home," she said. Another soror of hers was developing a local talk show, so she thought she could live off of her L.A. riches for a time, help her friend, and rejuvenate her sense of connection to people.

"I am a Bmore boy. I went to Coppin State and I am a radiologist. I work for a great hospital out in Montgomery County, but it's too damn expensive to live out there, so I came back home. My family is here and the houses are cheap." Why was I telling her so much? "Most of my friends from D.C. were coming up here to party anyway, so I figured I'd be ahead of the trend and make new

Baltimore my home. So far so good—my house is great and there's a lot to do. Baltimore will be the next hot place to live in the D.C. metro."

"You may have to keep hope alive on Baltimore beating D.C. for amenities, but I am with you that the city is much more metropolitan than it was when I was growing up," said Alecia. "The truth is I think like any city, having some money in your pocket makes it hot. My parents have been here all their lives, and there is so much they haven't seen just because financially it was out of reach. Part of me is excited that I can show them new Baltimore, but another part is sad that money matters that much."

Alecia told me she rented an apartment at Clipper Mill with floor-to-ceiling windows, lofty ceilings, and Sub-Zero appliances. The pool at Clipper Mill was consistently voted one of the best pools in the city. So much care was taken with the new developments that you just knew the city planned to flush old residents out and pump in young professionals by the boatload.

"Late at night," she said, "it is so easy for me to forget that I am in Baltimore. I stand at my front window and take in the lights of the city and the beautiful lights of the pool below. Where I am now is so different from my parents' row house. I am starting to really like new Bmore."

We talked the rest of the night while people were coupling off, hooking up, or leaving because their ideal match was nowhere in sight. Alecia was nestled deeply among the couch cushions and she was almost asleep. I told her that I was about to bounce.

Alecia looked around and said, "I think my ride may have disappeared for the night."

"You need me to drop you somewhere?" I asked.

"No. I'll just make myself nice and comfortable here on this fine leather couch," Alecia said as she stretched her legs out on the sofa.

It was about 3:00 a.m., and I knew that my boy Tug was not letting Brianna leave without breakfast, so I told Alecia to follow me.

"I know you don't think you got it like that."

I shook my head and grinned. "I gave up on gaming women years ago. If I wanted to seduce you, there would be no question. You'd know." At that she took my arm and I took her to the second-floor guest room. Once there, I graciously opened the door and let her walk in. My boy's house was bad. Every inch had been custom-decorated. This was the Africa room, with statues from Tug's trips with his job at the State Department, and linens and rugs of exotic fibers and patterns.

"This is kind of hot. I did not know that Tug had this in him," she said.

"Much better than the couch downstairs, I am sure. You will be thinking of me fondly in the morning as you roll over in the Egyptian cotton." Alecia laughed and gave me a little shove out the door.

"Thanks, brother Celin, for your sleep intervention, but you've got to go." Alecia had her hands clasped in front of her in mock reverence, and she smiled at me; just for a second I think I blushed. She was fun and easy to be around, and things had not been easy with a woman in a while. She shut the door and I took my drunken ass down to the fine leather couch to sleep.

In the a.m. Tug's house was a flurry of activity. Those too drunk to go home the night before were grabbing bottles of water and heading out to their cars. Strangers who were now lovers did the awkward dance similar to kids being forced to play nice with new cousins—knowing that you were supposed to like them but not sure if you actually do. Tug and Brianna finally emerged from his room. Brianna looked refreshed and comfortable wrapped in Tug's bathrobe. Tug was so happy to have her still here. He was shuffling around the kitchen to make her breakfast, all the while catering to her every fancy. *Could this really be a love match?* I wondered. Finally, Alecia made her way down the stairs. Her hair was loose and sprang up all around her head in a perfect circle. She had on some pajamas she'd found in the room. As she eased her way up to the kitchen island, she waved to us all and asked if it was okay that she'd used the PJs. Tug, said "You'd have to ask Celin, because those are his go-to pair for his tipsy nights." Alecia actually blushed and gestured at me like she didn't know. I told her it was cool, but she'd have to make sure that they didn't smell like berries and stuff because the ladies wouldn't appreciate that much.

"You nasty like that? Doing women at your boy's house?"

"Nope," I said. "It takes a special lady to get in my pants. Trust that I don't need Tug's place to get laid." I was getting a strong friend vibe from Alecia, but it could possibly be more.

When your man is dating a chick, more than likely you will spend a great deal of your time with one of her friends. By about the third time we all conveniently go out, usually I have asked my boy to let the sister know that I have moved, but with Alecia I did not mind having to take care of the third wheel. She was so fucking real and she just wanted to have a good time. Things between us weren't terribly romantic—just chill. She laughed at my jokes, and I was crazy about her sharp wit. The writer in her came out often, and the way she could describe a crazy club outfit, a brother's sad pickup line, or another call from her overly worried mom would have me in pain from laughing. Sometimes I caught Tug and Brianna looking at us like we had taken over the date.

One night we were all sitting around enjoying Alecia's latest greatest idea, sorbet covered in champagne, when the conversation turned to sex. Tug was making the point that most women did not know what good sex was. In his mind most women held on to romantic notions and images from their favorite movies and books. Few women had put in time with partners and porn—the only ways to really step up your skills. Brianna was making a case for just having natural ability. Some people were sexually gifted and others were just going to get by. I agreed with Tug that great sex comes from intense, hands-on study. Alecia was just quietly taking it all in. When I finally asked her what she thought, she said that she was in the middle. Very pointedly she said, "Look, we are all born with a degree of sexual knowledge and desire, but we mature, and experiences and knowledge tweak it a bit. I think plea-sure comes in many forms. You can't be shy in bed."

All night new debates popped up: reparations or no repara-tions, *Jeffersons* vs. *Good Times,* the state of hip-hop, and on and on. Eventually Tug got tired of getting beaten up by the ladies and he grabbed Brianna and they went off to bed. I told Alecia that if she was ready to go, she did not have to stay late to keep me com-pany. I was spending the night to go golfing in the morning with Tug. She said that she was fine and in no mood to go home to her empty loft. She told me that if I wanted to go to bed, that was okay; she was just going to go and study Tug's film collection and pick something to lull her to sleep. I wasn't ready to go to sleep ei-ther, so I decided to join the movie brigade. Alecia was in the mood to take the night way back with a Vanity classic, *The Last Dragon,* or take on the biggest challenge ever—the *Breakin'* movies. I was more into digging into the nineties flicks, a Spike Lee Joint or maybe even a Tarantino. Alecia said that she knew all of Spike's movies by heart, and plus we'd already resolved all of the great injustices against black people earlier in the evening. As far as Tarantino went, all she wanted to see was *Jackie Brown*—his best work, in her opinion. But alas, there was *Reservoir Dogs* next to *Pulp Fiction*, and absolutely no *Jackie Brown*. Alecia shook her head in amazement. "We are really going to have to take that brother's black card. No *Jackie Brown,* but he has the full Reese Witherspoon catalog."

I laughed, but I must admit *Election* was a funny-ass movie. I told Alecia to go back and sit down; I saw a movie I was sure she would love. She gave me that "yeah, right" look and planted her-self on the couch. I put the DVD on and couch-dived right next to her. As she stretched out, she said, "Let's see if you know what I like."

"I knew how to please you from day one."

As the movie title came up Alecia let out a loud "Ha." I knew that she'd love this one: it was the black single person's hope film—*Love Jones.*

The movie held up well; of course it did—Nia Long was fine as hell. Alecia seemed to especially enjoy the parts with the chick who used to be on *Ally McBeal*. What happened to her? As the final credits rolled up the screen, I jumped up to grab another movie. Alecia grabbed my arm, and I fell on top of her. "Look," she said, "what are we doing?"

I gave her the "huh" look, which I'd perfected over many years of not really knowing what women are talking about most of the time. The "huh" look gets you more info before you can incriminate yourself.

She went on, "We have been doing this safe friend thing for a while now, but it is getting a little boring. I want to fuck you. Have wanted to from the moment we met. I thought you'd notice and take the lead, but obviously that's my job. What do you think right now?"

Right then I was thinking *Daaammmmnnn*, but that wasn't exactly what she wanted to hear. Of course I thought Alecia was beautiful, and yes, I had thoughts about her—her mouth game, what her lower back looked like, and why the hell didn't she have a man? But I really liked her as a person, so I decided to chill and just be friendly and see what happened.

This is what happened.

By the time I'd finally gathered up my thoughts to answer, Alecia had already started to work her hands along my back under my shirt and lock her legs around me. I had planned to say, *I think you are a beautiful woman, and of course I have had thoughts about us. I am not one to take up something not offered, though, and I was cool to just be your friend. If you want to take it to the next level, we can do that. How about a real date tomorrow night?*

But I took too long because Alecia was already trying to figure out how to undo my pants. There is something about a hot chick fiddling with your pants that makes you kind of forget about appropriateness. Alecia slid from underneath me and jumped on top. She told me, "If you're scared, then end it now, because it is only going to get more live." Alecia removed my shirt and pants and ground her hips into mine. I was losing it. My dick was begging to be free and Alecia was not letting me touch her or remove any of her clothes. This was her scene and my only role was to comply. The next thing I knew Alecia had removed the elastic headband from her hair. She told me that I was not doing a good job of keeping my hands to myself so it was her job to help me. Alecia positioned my arms above my head and wrapped the band tightly around my wrists. The fabric dug into my skin, and Alecia warned me not to move too much or else it would chafe. The scenario had flipped and Alecia was calling the shots.

She stood up and pushed me to the floor, then commanded me to stand up and follow her into the bedroom. What the fuck was this? I was being bitched out by a 120-pound chick! The smart thing would have been to yell and wake the house up. But my man would have seen only what he wanted to see—me handling my business—and not a chick on some *Terminator* shit. I had to man up and ride this one out wherever it took me.

In the bedroom Alecia sat me down in the desk chair. She tied a scarf around my ankles, making me totally vulnerable to her every whim. I watched as she paced the room. She removed her clothes, and her body was bangin'. Alecia had a dancer's body—very petite and toned. Clearly a body that was worked on daily, inside and out. While she paced she explained to me what was going on. She'd been sensing the last few times that we hung out that I wanted to get with her, and because I never made a move it was apparent that it was her job to take over and teach me how to control a situation from start to finish.

As punishment for not taking the lead the way a man was supposed to, I was to please her totally tonight; I was her slave. She went over to the desk behind me, and I heard her search around in the drawer and then close it. Alecia came around and stood in front of me with a pair of scissors in her hand. The tip of the scissors made its way up my inner thigh as Alecia cut away my boxers. The cold metal, combined with anticipation, had me on the edge of the chair.

Once the remnants of my shorts hit the floor Alecia placed the scissors on the floor next to her. With her back turned to me she knelt down in between my legs. I loved the view of her perfect ass pointed in my direction. It was impossible for me to touch myself, but I needed some release, so I worked my thighs from left to right, lightly massaging my hard dick, which was throbbing against my belly. Just when I thought she was moving to ride me, Alecia propelled herself into a full-on handstand, her pussy right in my face. Like a good slave, I leaned into her as she spread her legs into a wide V to accommodate my tongue. I worked that pussy out, first sucking on the lips and then flicking my tongue over her clit. Just for good measure I teased Alecia by putting my tongue deep into her pussy, causing her to squirm under the pressure. Her pussy glistened, and I knew that my "master" was losing her grip. Alecia knew it too. She brought her legs into her chest and righted herself. A smile crossed Alecia's face as if to say, *You almost won.*

I assumed that because I had proven myself worthy, Alecia would set me free to be pleased. That would not be the case. She stood before me and all of a sudden she raised her foot and kicked me square in the chest. The blow flipped me and the chair onto the bed behind me. I rolled off the chair, and Alecia leapt like a superhero from the floor to the bed and landed with her knees hard on the middle of my chest. I curled up from the impact. What the fuck was all of this? This woman really liked it rougher than anyone I'd ever encountered. Some of the things she'd done to me were definitely criminal, and I still was not convinced that any of it was "fun." Alecia stretched me out flat on the bed and straddled my waist. She leaned over me and looked in my eyes while stroking my chest. Her hands felt like heaven, and all I wanted was for her to wrap them around my dick. Alecia looked at me and said, "All you have to do is tell me how much you want me to hurt you, and I will do it . . . anything. I will do it." Mesmerized by the sensation of her wet pussy on my skin, I told her what she wanted to hear. In the darkness of that room I told her to hurt me.

My whispers were falling on deaf ears because Alecia did not respond. I said it again a little louder: "Please hurt me." Each time I said it she rubbed her pussy harder on my dick. I said it even louder, and that was when Alecia yelled at me that I needed to yell like the bitch I was and she would give me what I wanted. Tug and Brianna were in the room next door, and I knew they were hearing all of this. "Yell like the bitch you are," she said again, even louder. I just stared, and that was when it happened. Alecia grabbed my nipples in between her thumbs and index fingers and twisted them so hard that I lost my breath. It was then that I yelled out, "*Sssshhhhhiiiittttt!*" in the darkness. While twisting my nipples Alecia eased her pussy onto my dick. Her pussy sucked me in and held on tight. The stinging in my nipples coupled with her ability to deep-massage my dick with the inside of her vagina made me cum in seconds. The orgasm was so strong that my knees popped up and bounced her off the bed and into the wall. Every inch of my body was cumming, and I could not stop the convulsions. The only way that I could calm my body was to roll over onto my stomach and tuck my knees under me.

In my head all I could think was, *What the hell was that and when can it happen again?* Alecia picked herself off the floor and was laughing. All she could say as she removed her headband from my hands and the scarf from my feet was that I was so good. I rolled over onto my back, and Alecia lay down next to me, rested her head on my chest, and said, "You are now my bitch." My chest was still pumping up and down, and as much as I tried I could not get it together. This woman had rendered me powerless. Alecia had showed me that I was vulnerable, but as much as I loved the pleasure, I hated the pain. I forced her over on her back and I lay on top of her. I kissed her hard, biting her lips and cheek. I wanted her to feel what I felt and to have evidence all over her body that I'd been there. She moved to push me off her, and I smacked her in the face to make her submit. Alecia smiled and said, "You finally get it. How did that feel?"

I looked into this woman's eyes—a woman who had put me

through one of the most physically exhausting nights of my life—and I told her that I no longer felt like her bitch.

That was the beginning of my awakening. It's like your first alcoholic drink or drug hit; you don't really understand all of the fuss until you experience it. Alecia and I continued like that for the next six months. She would break into my place at night and use handcuffs, zip cuffs, stockings, and even harnesses to render me helpless. I started to smack her around more in bed and really get off on attacking her from behind outside work, at home, or basically anywhere I knew that she was not expecting me to be. Our sex was satisfying because we were both willing participants. Alecia schooled me in the game we were playing: only do it with willing participants (she said she saw it in my eyes the first day we met that regular women bored me), establish limits (no more scissors for me and no punching for her), and be innovative (I was getting extremely good with hot wax, stickpins, and scratching).

One day Alecia received a lead on a hot new writing gig for a television show out of New York. She'd helped her friend as much as she could on her Baltimore project, and I knew she was itching to jump right back in with the in-crowd she'd come back home to escape. Before she left she introduced me to some Web sites and clubs that would feed my needs until I could find her replacement. Replacing Alecia would be hard because she'd grown to represent even more of the perfect package to me. Did I love Alecia? I really don't know, but sometimes people are placed in your life just to let you know that love is still possible when you've started to seriously doubt it.

The day she left for New York, while we stood there in front of her moving van with our foreheads touching, I knew that I was going to be lonely again. Our bond was more than love or lust—it was a secret understanding that we could have whatever we wanted, even if it meant bruising our bodies or egos. We made the ultimate sacrifice for each other each time we came together. I was going to miss her, and I hoped that she would miss me too. Alecia stood on her toes and kissed me softly on the lips. She hugged me and smiled, and then without warning she grabbed my dick hard and jumped into the van. All I could do was smile and hope like hell she hated New York.

It has been two months since Alecia left, and she "simply loves" New York. We talk about once a week on the phone and we email often, but I get the sense that she is trying to build something in a new city and that it's best that I try to move on. She always tells me that she misses me, and the photos that she sends are beyond naughty, but we both are mature enough to know that sometimes even good situations can run their course. So now I am out there looking for a new play partner. Getting chicks has never been a problem, but landing a chick who is into real S&M activity is hard. The Web sites feel cold, and frankly, the women are not that hot. The sex club didn't work for me because there were too many rules and too many dudes looking for male action.

I did meet Amy there, who has become a placeholder. In the club Amy is cool, but as soon as we step out, she becomes a married mom of two with a high-profile politico husband. I have met regular chicks that I thought I could convert. Most were good with the soft stuff—spanking, blindfolds, and scarves—but when I stepped it up they lost the ability to answer their phones. One woman, Karen, I just happened to bump into during a shopping run one Saturday, and before I could say hello I saw her run in the opposite direction. One chick seemed cool with my penchant for roughness for a while. Belinda loved the kink and the pain. She even liked when I would attack her by surprise. Things were going well until one day we were sitting around her place watching the news and the reporter started talking about a series of attacks on women in southwest Baltimore. The dude was randomly targeting and tackling women by rubbing himself against them and running off. I noticed Belinda turned up the volume on the television and slid away from me on the couch. For two weeks she questioned where I was going and what I was doing. When she finally asked me straight out if I was getting my stalker jollies from innocent women I knew that it was time for the relationship to end. Belinda was conflicted.

Passionate one second and calling the cops the next. Definitely not my dream girl.

Alecia spoiled me because she was not only my freak but also my ideal girl. It has been hard trying to find a replacement. Are there no witty, attractive women who like an occasional cheese grater spanking?

Darwin

Love Dove bars? Can't get enough of Oreos? I am looking to create my very own tasty treat. I am a 22-year-old white guy who loves black chicks. The darker the better. No Vanessa Williamses, Halle Berrys, or Beyoncés need to apply. I am into the Naomis, Mo'Niques, and Kenya Moores of the world. TS611

am a white dude who only dates black women. Everything about them turns me on—their swagger, their confidence, the smoothness of their skin, and most importantly the curves, from the lips to the hips—perfection. I am a true lover. Not a white dude looking for "something different" or just wanting to brag to my boys about all the exotic chicks I have been with. My love is based on where I'm from and how I was raised. On the real, I am probably blacker than many of you reading this shit. I am not some strange white motherfucker who fantasizes about big asses, thick lips around my dick, and seeing my white cum on black skin. Naw, I just am keeping it real. I am a real nigga from Cherry Hill, and after growing up in that neighborhood I couldn't help loving all things black because that was all I saw.

I have two brothers—my brother Jaime and I have the same father, Chris, who is white, and my brother Marco has a black father, Carl. Chris disappeared years ago after Jaime was born, leaving my moms with a drug habit and two little boys. Carl stepped in and helped my moms through rehab, got us an apartment, and then eventually married my moms. Carl is my dad and his family is my family. I respect that black man.

All through school I had to prove that I was the blackest white guy you know. Most thought I was trying too hard with clothes, the music, the way I talk, and shit, but on the real that was me. I was no Towson or White Marsh suburb motherfucker trying to "represent." What you see is what you get. And based on whose eyes are looking at me, I am either the coolest white boy ever or the most confused young man ever (according to one of my white uncles).

I met this girl in high school named Kari, who would clown me on the daily and say stuff like my hair was too long and my nose was too pointy and why did I talk like that and why couldn't I just leave because I did not belong here. She traveled with a group of chicks that laughed at all of her insults. One day I just couldn't take all the questions and shit from her anymore. I told her if she really wanted to know about white people to pick up a fucking book and stop asking me dumb-ass questions. Her face as well as the faces of her entourage dropped. The class laughed, and even Mr. Johnson, our biology teacher, held back a chuckle before saying that I needed to chill on that type of language in the class. He didn't tell me I was wrong, but that I phrased it wrong and shit. I knew I needed to work on that.

At the start of senior year, Kari was on my lab team and she stopped being all up in my ass about being white and really focused on our work. I always liked my science classes because of all the gore of checking out the insides of shit and playing around with the knives. But Kari tied our lab work into greater things. Things that I didn't really think about. How the way that I enjoyed dissecting frogs and learning about body parts could turn into a career down the road where I could do the same shit on humans and develop new pills and other treatments to make people healthy. She said that she wanted to focus on research involving women's health because there was an article in the *Sun* that said women don't get great medical care because most drugs and treatments were developed and tested on men. This bitch was on some whole new crazy shit now. What happened to the insensitive Kari with her dumb and bigoted bullshit?

One day Kari and I had to stay after school to clean the lab. As I was collecting tool kits from each table, I asked Kari why she was getting all serious and shit on a nigga.

"You need to slow up with the N word for real . . that's not cute." She glared at me. I was trying to cut down, I really was. "We are seniors and time is running out and I have to get my shit together. High school is coming to an end, and I refuse to be trapped in Bmore. I'm doing everything I can to get to the next level."

I was confused for a moment, trying to figure out what she was talking about, and then it hit me: college. "You really talking about going to college?" I said.

Kari stopped wiping the tabletop. "Yes. What else is there? Are you telling me, Darwin, that you don't know what you'll be doing once we get out of here? Damn, Darwin, there is more to life than living in Cherry Hill and getting a chicken box." I knew that shit already. Kari just liked embarrassing a ni— brother.

Kari sat on a stool and said, "I just don't want to get stuck here with nothing. My sister Leelee was doing well, but she had a little too much fun and now she doesn't have the grades, money, or time to do anything else but work." Kari's older sister, Leelee, had just found out that she was pregnant and that because she didn't work full-time she didn't have any benefits and had to turn to the state for help. Leelee was twenty years old and was starting the welfare struggle that her mom was still a slave to all these years later. Kari was not going to make those same mistakes. She was going to college, and on the real, she had to figure it out on her own. That's why she'd slowed up on the clowning and acting out. As much as she enjoyed making my "pimply white ass squirm," that dumb shit wasn't going to help her when she graduated.

Kari then asked me about what I planned to do after graduation. The truth is that a motherfucker didn't know. I guess I always assumed that Carl would hook me up with a job installing cable. My moms never worked a day since she met Carl and we had a nice enough place to stay, hot gear, and vacations. That seemed like a good job. Kari said that that sounded cool and all but what was Carl going to do when he got too old to climb ladders and hang from people's windows? What if people decided to go with some underground phone wire cable shit? "Not to dog your dad out, dude," she said, "but what is he going to do when that shit goes away? I think about that kind of stuff all the time." She continued, "Leelee was smart enough to get a decent job with a credit card company in their customer service department, but without a degree, she is going to work harder and longer to move up. My sister will be fine, Darwin, but she is going to struggle. I know that life does not have to be shit, and I just decided it's up to me to make sure that I am okay."

We talked some more while finishing up the lab. And when we left school we continued on talking about our futures and the lack of futures for a lot of our boys. "Little Mike was shot over there at the BP last month. Were you friends?" Kari asked.

"No," I said. "We had some classes together, but I remember he ran with Cokie. Cokie got shot, what, a year ago?" Kari nodded and looked away.

"The funny thing is," she said, "Cokie didn't get shot for the coke he had on him daily, but some dumb girl got him shot over some shoes he bought for her."

"Yeah," I said. "We all tripped over that one. What makes you want to kill someone over some damn shoes?"

"I don't know," said Kari. "It's hard to tell where the bullets are coming from lately." She paused. "You seem to stay out of the shit, though, Darwin."

Honestly, I didn't really know how I had been able to not get caught up. I knew a lot of my boys were slingers, and trust me, I have had more than enough close encounters with cops. I guess the drug shit didn't appeal to me because I'd seen up close and personal what my moms went through, and the gang shit was not happening because Carl wasn't having that shit. He said the only gang that I needed to worry about was the "Clinksdale family gang . . . where it was easy to get in and hard as hell to get out."

Once my friend Dre and I got picked up by the cops for loitering. Carl came into the station in a huff to pick me up because this shit had taken him off his route. He glared at me and then got himself together and thanked the cop for calling him first. He asked if he could "take his boy home." Once we were in the car he told me how lucky I was that the cop on duty was a friend. Then for the next twenty minutes I had to hear how lucky I am and that I didn't need any bullshit charges on my record. How I would not ruin my future and how he had invested too much in me for me to be a fuckup. Carl ended the conversation like he ended all of his speeches: "I love you, and don't let this be a pattern." I guess I wasn't a real fuckup because it was not an option.

Kari and I kicked it a lot after that. I learned that she was the middle child of five and that she often felt that no one really cared what happened to her. Her dad still came around, but he had remarried and moved to Philly. She made it clear that she wasn't a hater. Kari knew that her parents weren't happy together and it was best that they'd divorced. She only wondered why he'd moved so far away. The upside, though, was that she got to spend summers in Philly, and her stepmom was a stylist for some groups up there, so she got to go to all the hot concerts and there were always famous people stopping by the house for their gear. Kari made me think about things differently, and I really saw a whole lot of shit that I was blind to before. One night we were just kicking it out in front of my building when Kari's girls walked by. She got up and went to talk to her girls, and I really got a chance to look at her. Kari was tall and thin with skin the color of night. She kept her hair natural and her smile was fire. Her gear was always tight via her stepmom. All these weeks I had never really seen Kari as a girl—just my lab partner. But now Kari was a cutie, and I was about to be hooked.

Kari came back and sat down next to me, and oddly, a brother was a little nervous. As she went on and on about her girl and the girl's boyfriend and how she was stupid to keep trusting his ass, all I could do was stare at her lips. I wondered how they felt and if she'd even let me touch her face. Suddenly the smiling lips stopped moving and Kari asked me, "What the fuck are you staring at? Do I got something in my teeth?"

"No, I was just looking," I said. Her eyes narrowed, and she looked at me and said, "Darwin, you not catching feelings, are you?"

"Naw, not at all," I said. "I just like what I see."

"Really. What do you want to do with what you see?"

"Anything you want. What are you up for?"

Right then she leaned in and kissed me. It was all banana gloss. The best I'd ever experienced.

She pulled back and said, "About damn time . . . I was starting to think your punk ass was gay." Naw, not gay, just a virgin, but she didn't need to know that.

The next week was all about school, homework, kicking it with my boys, and hanging out with Kari on the stoop until sundown. Then we'd walk down to the park and make out. Kari had rules:

- I could kiss her anywhere.

- She was not sucking my dick.

- There wasn't going to be any intercourse.

- She would jack me off on occasion, but not every time.

- And most importantly . . . there was no butt sex in her future.

I never let her know that feeling her up was enough for me because that was about as far as I had ever gone. She was masterly with her hands and when she would place her hands around my dick and stroke me I thought I would bust within seconds. Kari liked the power she had over me and I liked that she already knew what to do. One night she told me that she was finally ready to let me hit it, but I had to use a condom and it couldn't be in a damn park. I told her that my moms was volunteering at Marco's school that week and no one would be home during the day. If she didn't mind ditching after first period we could go back to my place. She smiled and said that I had a date.

The next day I made sure that my moms was going to be out all day. Before leaving for school I cleaned my room a little because my moms had told me a long time ago that chicks don't like dirt. I walked into first period and saw Kari and sat down next to her. She mouthed hi and the teacher, Mr. Hite, went on and on for forty-five minutes about shit that right then and there meant absolutely nothing. Did he know that I was going up in a piece in about an hour? Did he know that a chick had finally said yes?

As soon as the bell rang Kari and I jetted for the building's side doors. I held her hand on the way into my building. Generally, I am not a hand-holder, but for some reason I felt it was the right thing to do. Once inside my apartment I asked Kari if she wanted something to drink and she said no. She wanted to see my room. There wasn't much to see. I shared it with my brother Jaime so there were two twin beds, an old dresser that we shared, and a closet busting at the seams. I was nervous as hell so I launched into a crazy conversation about all of the posters that I had collected over the years. I was into this whole thing about how I'd caught Talib Kweli one night leaving Ram's Head and how cool he was about me bugging him and shit when Kari said, "I know you didn't bring my ass in here to talk about posters." No, I hadn't, but I wasn't real sure how to move on. Luckily, I did not have to wait long for the next move.

Kari pulled me close and told me to close my eyes. Slowly she moved her nose all over my face. She barely touched me but was close enough that I could smell her hair and lip gloss. She told me that she wanted me to really feel her. Kari then took her nose down onto my neck and with her lips began to kiss me softly. Once she came back up to my lips to kiss me it wasn't the anxious or inexperienced kisses that I was used to. Her game was tighter than that; she was trying to seduce me and it was working.

Suddenly Kari pulled back and looked me directly in my eyes and said, "You know what's coming next . . . are you ready?"

"Hell yeah," I responded.

"Naw," she said, "don't give me boyhood bullshit. I know you can do it—at least I hope so. I need to know if you are really ready for what this means for me." At that I had to take a step back. This was no jump-off. Kari was making it clear to me that this was going to be a relationship and that I had to take this shit seriously. At that moment I had to decide if I was going to be a boy and say something slick and keep things moving or if I was going to man up.

As Kari looked at me for an answer, I told her, "Being with you has been the highlight of my year—maybe even my life—and I would never do anything to make you regret your decision."

At that she laughed and said, "That was corny-ass shit, but cute. Did you bring any condoms?"

"Yeah, I got that covered."

Kari kissed me hard on my lips and said, "By the way, thanks for being so great."

Amazingly, the girl with the smart mouth and who knew everything about everything switched gears and allowed me to take control. Kari lay back on my bed and I lay on top of her. I lifted her shirt and kissed her belly. I worked my way up from her belly past her tits to suck on her neck. I was so nervous to not push too hard or do anything she was not comfortable with. We developed this way of speaking without words where she would simply move me where she wanted me to be and I knew that things were okay. I felt her grab the back of my head and lower my mouth onto her tits. They were small and firm. She pushed her bra up so that I could get to her nipples and then unhooked the clasp on it so that it could just be torn away. I stopped for a minute to look at her. She was gorgeous. Better than any video, magazine, or fantasy. She was real and she was mine. I pulled my shirt off. She ran her fingers through my hair and laughed. She said that she'd never thought she'd be with a guy with hair longer than hers. Kari giggled and said I'd have to work on getting a cut if I wanted to be her man.

At that moment she could have asked me to paint myself green and split in half and I would have done it.

Once she was totally undressed, I asked her to stand up so that I could look at her. As clueless as I was about all of this, I knew that I did not want to forget this moment. I wanted this burned into my mind like my moms's smile and the lyrics of my favorite song—important shit. Kari was so tall and thin and everything about her was beautiful to me, from her fly-ass short haircut to the thin gold cross around her neck and the small flowers painted on her toes. She was cool as shit and I wanted her to know it. I got on my knees in front of her and I kissed the side of her hips. I parted the lips of her pussy and started licking her. I licked her softly all over her pussy and wherever I was when I heard her say my name I knew that I needed to lick there more. I was new to this, but I had heard enough from boys to know that her moans meant "do more," and I was going to do as much as Kari wanted. Kari was enjoying it because she held on to the back of my head and would not let me move away. She was pushing me in deeper exactly where she wanted me to be.

Finally I knew that it was time. I leaned Kari back on the bed and removed my clothes. Her skin was so soft and she smelled like vanilla. I looked at her and she looked at me and I knew that I wanted to see her like this forever. We started to kiss again and then I jumped up. I went and grabbed the condom from my dresser and ripped it open. I placed it on the tip of my dick, and then Kari said, "Let me do it." I stood and she slowly rolled it down my dick. She massaged every inch and made sure to keep me hard. I stretched out on the bed and she came and laid down on top of me. Carefully she placed me inside her. I had never felt anything that warm and tight. Her pussy sucked me up and it felt like nothing I'd ever experienced. *Is this why dudes lose their minds? Is this what niggas be writing songs about?* At that moment I finally got it. And it was as good as I'd expected.

Kari bounced on top of me and she would occasionally roll her body back and forth. I enjoyed the view. With her eyes closed and her fingers digging deeply into the sides of my thighs, I knew that she was enjoying herself. I wanted to feel her and slow down the pace a bit, so I pulled her forward when it was time for me to take control. We rolled over and I began to move in and out of her slowly and deliberately. I had seen in a flick one time that there are areas in a woman's body that you can better reach if you are more deliberate in your stroke. I was in her ear telling her how much I wanted her, how good this felt, and how much I wanted to be like this forever. Kari must have liked what I was saying, or maybe it was my dick, because she began to push up against me harder and with her stronger thrusts and the visual of her breasts bouncing beneath me I lost it. I came so hard that I had to pull out immediately. The touch of her fingers, her breath on my skin and even the tightness of her pussy were causing my body to tingle way after the fact. All I could do was pull her close to me and with her back to my lips I kissed her skin softly. I would never forget the major gift she'd given me.

Kari and I kicked it for the remainder of our senior year. During that time we grew to love each other, and there was no one else that I trusted or wanted to be around more than her. My family treated her like another relative, and eventually Kari's family stopped looking at me suspiciously when they realized that I wasn't trying to take advantage of her and, more importantly, I wasn't going anywhere. This for me was the real deal, and I honestly could not think of being with another girl.

I had picked up my grades, but the truth is there really was no money in the house for me to go to college. And because I had waited so long to do better, scholarships were pretty much out of the question. I was stressed. For the first time I was actually concerned about what was happening next.

There was a good chance that I would be left behind in Baltimore and Kari would be off doing her thing on a campus. She did great on her SATs. Colleges were calling her to ask her to apply and she went to reception after reception for schools vying for her attention. In the end she decided to attend a women's college in North Carolina because she got a full four-year scholarship. All she had to do was keep her grades up and work a campus job. Kari was elated, but I was not.

Don't get me wrong. She was my girl and I knew that she had worked long and hard to get into college. She more than deserved it, but why did she have to go so far? I knew that she was going to be swooped up by some older college dude looking to run game and I didn't expect her to turn down a guy with a chance at a future for a nigga back in Bmore with no job and no plan.

I was a little surprised that nothing was really happening for me. My grades weren't great, but I had maintained at least a 2.0 for most of the four years. I had stayed out of trouble with the law and even had a guidance counselor and teacher write really good recommendations for me, but still no real takers. I was wait-listed at Maryland, Towson said flat-out no, and Hopkins might as well have sent their letter back with a huge "Nigga, please" on the outside. The only school that said yes was Allegheny, but there were no dollars attached and I didn't want to be in the mountains anyway. I just checked it off because it was first on the list for Maryland schools. It's funny—you always hear growing up, especially where I live, that it is so easy for white people. That we can get whatever we want. I think on a subconscious level I thought that might be true. I was testing the shit out of that theory now. Really, I think it's more about what you have in your pockets than skin color, because no one was cutting me any breaks and it sure was not coming easy.

One night Kari and I were at her house making arrangements for prom. The whole school was hyped because the Club Queen, K-Swift from 92Q, was mixing at our prom, and we planned to get our shake off all night. Kari's moms wanted to make sure that she had the hottest prom night ever, like something from that MTV show *Sweet Sixteen*. So while she went on and on about a stretch Hummer and dinner on the harbor and a marching band on the lawn (did she know that we lived in the 'hood?), I was only halfway listening because I was stressed about my lack of a plan. Kari asked me why I was so distant. Of course I said, "No reason"; I did not want to ruin her excitement over prom. She gave me that look that she always gives me when she knows that I am bullshitting her. I 'fessed up and told her that my shit was just not falling in place like hers. I didn't have anything going on and that all this end-of-school talk was making me even more anxious.

We went back to her bedroom to talk. Her mother said we could be back there as long as the bedroom door stayed open. I lay across Kari's bed and she lay down next to me. She said, "I thought Allegheny said yes."

"Yeah, but without a scholarship, nothing can jump off."

Kari asked, "Where else did you apply?" I ran the list down for her, and she just shook her head at me. "Are you that damn dumb?" she said. "None of those schools need you as a student, so they aren't going to do a thing for you. You need to apply to an all-black school, an HBCU. They need you to keep getting that government money and appear fair in the admission. Work the damn system," Kari said. "Meet me after school tomorrow and I'll go through my college guide to pick some schools for you to apply to. You are way late to the game, but there still may be a chance for you to get accepted somewhere in the fall." Once again Kari had a nigga's back.

The next day I headed over to Carl's job to help him with a few of his installations. Kari's moms had made it clear to me the day before that I was going to need some dollars for prom night, and Carl promised me $50 for every install that I did. He was getting tired of all the climbing and crawling, so he would go in and greet the customers and I would run around and do the heavy lifting. I was learning the business and making money, so it wasn't a bad deal for me. It was after 6:00 p.m. and I kept checking my cell for Kari's call. There were no missed calls or messages. Usually she called me as soon as she hit the door, and I was especially anxious that day because she was going to do the college thing with me. I hadn't even been able to sleep the night before thinking that I was a dumb-ass for not knowing this to begin with and also being excited that maybe I could go to school in NC near Kari.

I called Kari's cell and she didn't pick up, so I decided to just go over. When I finished the last installation with Carl, he dropped me off at Kari's building. There were people in front of the doorway. Carl put the car in park while I got out to see what was going down. I entered the building. People stood on the stairs talking nonstop about some shit that I didn't understand. Kari's apartment door was open and the place was filled with people. Kari's moms was on the couch and Kari's sister was fanning her. I looked around and I didn't see Kari. I headed back toward her bedroom but some dude hemmed me up. I shook him off and he stepped to me again and asked where I was going. Then I heard Leelee say, "That's Kari's boyfriend. Damn, Darwin, come here. I didn't see you come in." I sat down next to Leelee and I saw that Kari's moms was crying and hugging Kari's graduation picture. I knew something wasn't right.

"Leelee, where is Kari?" I asked. Leelee looked at me and the color drained from her face.

"Sweetie, you don't know? Kari was hit by a stray bullet on the way home from school today. She didn't make it."

It couldn't be true. Maybe they had the wrong person, or maybe they'd notified the wrong family—that had happened to my boy once—but when I looked around the room I saw that there were cops taking statements and even a few reporters taking notes. This shit was real. My boo was gone.

Kari's funeral was held at Graves Temple, one of the largest churches in the city. That day every politician, community activist, and area minister took to the pulpit to "decry the violence in the streets" and "celebrate a life cut short too soon." I thought it was all bullshit because none of them had known Kari or her family and most of them had never walked the streets of Cherry Hill. I knew for a fact that a few of the politicians had been blown up in the papers for not residing in the city but using their rental properties as their city address. Also, ministers who drive Maseratis and Bentleys definitely don't live in the 'hood, so what the fuck could they say to me? I was just getting hot sitting there listening to all of it. No wonder their programs and projects fail. They're not saying anything that is real.

Mr. Johnson, our biology teacher, was the last to say something. Mr. Johnson's five minutes said more than forty-five minutes of people who supposedly did this sort of thing for a living. He talked about Kari's fiery spirit, dedication to learning, and desire to help everyone that she met overcome their circumstances. Mr. Johnson said, "Kari got a lesson early on that none of us were perfect, but we were all placed here to pursue our personal best. Her encouragement made a difference in my classroom for many of my students, and hopefully her life story will be an inspiration to others." All of the students in the building stood up. We clapped our hands until it hurt. There were no more words that needed to be said. It was time to put my boo to rest.

My family did not go to the gravesite. My moms talked to all of us about how important it was to be helpful to Kari's family during this time, so she'd volunteered to oversee the repast. After the funeral my family went to Kari's apartment to get the house ready. At first I was hurt that I wouldn't be able to go to the cemetery, but my moms made a good point about this being something that Kari and her family would appreciate more—it was something we could do for them as a family. People started pouring in, and like most funerals there was all sorts of crazy talk going through the room: men talking shit about the Ravens, ladies complimenting one another on their dresses, and more insignificant shit being said that I could not wrap my mind around. They weren't talking or really feeling anything for Kari, though when the reporters' cameras were rolling these same people could not contain their sorrow. Kari's uncle Mikey even passed out during his interview on WBAL. That shit was going to be on YouTube. A few minutes before, he was sitting across from me sipping a Coors and talking about hitting Eldorado's later that night because Buffie the Body was in town. *Are you kidding me? Is this what these motherfuckers are thinking about?*

I couldn't take it anymore. I left the dining room and headed back to Kari's room. One of Kari's big-ass cousins made a move to stop me, but I saw Leelee tell him to leave me alone. Once inside I shut the door and fell on her bed. I looked at her ceiling and saw those damn glow-in-the-dark stars she talked about all the time. On her desk were all of the tiny-ass bears I'd won for her at the state fair because I couldn't get her one of the giant ones. On her coat hook was her book bag and her favorite jacket. Her sheets smelled like her, and being in her space calmed me down. I heard a knock on the door and Kari's moms entered the room. I sat up on the edge of the bed and she sat next to me. She said, "Darwin, I was never big on my girl's dating because I knew how dating made me have to grow up fast and then Leelee too. Kari was different than us, and she dodged that dating thing for a long time until a white boy snuck under her radar. I wanted her to end it, but she said that you were different . . . respectful of the things that I wanted for her. Thanks for loving and being good to my daughter." I didn't know what to say. The tears started coming and they wouldn't stop. Kari's moms held me close and rocked me, saying, "It's okay, baby, it's okay." She held my face in her hands and said,

"The hard work for you is just beginning. Take this as a sign that you must pull yourself up out of here. There is nothing left here for you other than your family, and they will go with you in your heart wherever you are. Take this." She went into Kari's backpack and pulled out a book as thick as a Bible. It was the college guide that Kari had been planning to go over with me the day she died. "I looked through it, and she had highlighted some schools for you to read about. You come over one week from now and we will start working on applications and essays. I know you can do it, your family on the other side of that door knows you can do it, and Kari knew you could do it. Now do it." She stood, ran her hands through my hair, and kissed the top of my head.

Four years later, I am a graduate of Hampton University. I majored in computers and information systems and I work for a technology firm specializing in smart-card solutions. Kari's moms definitely kept her promise to me all those years ago, and we worked for two weeks straight on my applications. She knew exactly what to say to catch the admissions office's attention. She told me to talk about my love of computers and exotic fish and to talk about the difficulties of growing up in Baltimore and how I saw education as my only hope. Kari's moms even went with me to a few of the local interviews and made sure that I was dressed right and knew interesting facts about each institution. I was accepted to Hampton, Howard, and Virginia State. Hampton and Virginia State offered provisional full rides (lots of on-campus work, summer remedial programs, and minimum grade requirements), but Hampton was near the beach.

College life was hard at first. I had to set my own rules in order to not get behind. I was the token boy on campus—the white guy who couldn't get in anywhere else who was slumming at Hampton for free. I chose to address it head-on when it came up, and during my freshman year that was quite often. My go-to was that I was happy as hell that I got in because I had fucked up in high school. Most of the haters let it go when I did not run away from the obvious. Dating was dubious for a while, but I got my swagger back and the hotties all wanted to give me a try.

On graduation day I had two families waiting for me: mine and Kari's. Kari's moms never gave up on me and would snap me back in place if she heard I wasn't doing what was right. There is not a day that passes that I am not thankful for Kari's influence on my life.

And that is why I love black women!

So I just moved back home and I need to get out and meet some people. I'm placing this ad in *TEASE* and it must've really been an eye-catcher because responses rolled in immediately. The editor, Destiny, sent me a reply directly, saying that the magazine is hosting a party and she has a teaser she'd like to introduce me to, although this friend only dated black men previously.

You know what, Destiny? Love comes in many flavors. It may be time to try a new scoop.

Destiny

Where My dogs At?

This week we are having an office debate over who is more down and dirty in relationships, men or women. The guys say men because it is physically hard for guys to be faithful. Most of the ladies say men as well. I tell them that I think women are worse because we control when men get sex, and because we're better liars than men when it comes to concealing something important. George, a graphic artist who has been married for more than twenty years, disagrees, and says that most women are faithful to their husbands if the men are halfway decent, while men will cheat on the most beautiful and successful woman just for some variety. I ask George straight up if he has ever cheated on Maxie and he says no (good answer), but he has thought about it, only dismissing it because he didn't want to disappoint Maxie.

Katina says, "All men are dogs and they either age out of the game or just get too damn tired to lie." Even Deanna chimes in, at which point we forward all the mag's phones to voice mail, because the *TEASE* newsroom is clearly heating up.

Deanna is taking the standpoint that both men and women need to work on loving one another better and that if we really loved our partners there would be no need for outside affairs. Deanna lives in Deanna Land, so we quickly move on to Sol for his opinion. Sol feels that women do cheat and lie in love, but they don't do it quite as much as guys and definitely not with the huge fuckup factor. Men get caught wrong often, public and big— ladies don't.

Felipe feels that it's a fifty-fifty split. "Guys are awful when it comes to love, and my female friends are just as scandalous. All of love is just a shitfest," according to Felipe.

Libby, our arts editor, feels that guys are definitely the worst in love. She is newly divorced and fighting with her ex over who should have their wedding photos (Who cares? You are not to-gether anymore), and she's more than a little bitter when it comes to guys. Libby's husband never communicated with her and was more interested in his bike than her. After three years of trying to get her husband to emote and pay attention, she came home from the paper to find their house empty and their dog gone. He'd left her and didn't discuss that with her either. We know where Libby stands without her saying a word.

And in all of my relationship drama, I know it isn't the bad men to blame, it's me standing in my own way. I've done my dirt in love—not calling guys back, seeing two friends, and dating my girl's ex—but I know to keep my transgressions to myself. I am alone because I have the hot panties for a guy with absolutely no time for or real interest in me (Denae) and am avoiding a guy will-ing to be a real boyfriend because I don't care enough to even get to know him better (Josh). Many a late night I have burned up the phone lines with my girl trying to find the magic pill to stop being so selfish, awful, and stupid. So while my co-workers don't need to know my personal business, I definitely know that women could be and often are the most treacherous when it comes to love.

In order to put the conversation to bed and get back to business, we each have to put out there the most awful thing we've ever done to a lover:

- *Libby.* She's done nothing wrong in love ever. It's pencil-dick bastards who keep tripping her up. (The girl needs therapy.)

- *Felipe.* He surprised a new guy with a threesome with Felipe's ex that he still secretly loved and hoped to eventually get back with. He thought it would be a permissible way to get some sex from the ex.

- *Katina.* Lied and said she was on her period over a vacation with a new guy because she was not feeling him anymore but still wanted to go to London on his tab.

- *Sol.* In college he took money from the wallet of a girl he was seeing just for sex to catch a cab to see another girl who was hotter—her sister.

- *George.* Maxie is the second woman that he asked to marry him within a week. He was seeing two women at the same time and the first girl turned him down. He really wanted to get married, asked both women, and only Maxie said yes.

- *Deanna.* She didn't say thank you for an expensive night out. (Deanna is stuck somewhere in the 1950s. Is she for real?)

It is now my turn and I don't even know where to start. Do I tell them that once I bit a guy on the dick purposely because I was tired of going down on him and he would not cum? Should I admit that I actually told a guy that I had gone gay because I did not want him to visit me when he came to town on business? Those times were pretty horrible, but all I could think of was the fact that I was really being terrible right now because I had seen Josh a few times around town and ducked out or avoided his glance and he had done absolutely nothing to deserve the treatment. The Josh thing is a little fresh and a few of the people in the office know about his flowers, so I give them the gay story.

After reviewing the stories we determine that maybe men and women are equally trifling, and that maybe we just need to treat one another with more respect. Is it possible that Deanna, who hasn't had a date since the invention of the cell phone, may be the most together of all of us?

> You are my slut and queen. There is no one who could love me the way that you do and I am thankful for that. I love you. TS309
>
> The hardness of you shakes me to the core. I love you because you love all of me. Not just my body but my mind too. I am yours. TS310

I have waited a long time to get married. When my friends were coupling off in their twenties I was starting to date. In my thirties many of them had added kids to the mix while I was trying out my first serious relationship. It wasn't until I turned the big four-oh that I decided it might be time to stop playing and put down some roots. For a few years I tried to convince twentysomethings that I was the man of their dreams: college-educated, successful, a homeowner, and child-free. They didn't bite. Then I tried out a few thirtysomethings, but they were too anxious to seal the deal and oftentimes didn't understand that I still needed my space. The forty-and-over set was scary for me because I wanted my own kids and not the burden of dealing with another man's. Still, I was surprised at how many forty-plus sisters were still out there with no marriages or children. These women were a great fit, but none of the love stories lasted for long. Most I lost to younger men (times were changing); a few were still trying to decide if they were straight or not (shouldn't you know by now?); and the rest just weren't willing to give up their lives to join mine.

My boys had warned me that the player would eventually get played, and it seemed that I was powerless to turn this hex around.

Here I was in my big-ass house out in Owings Mills with two luxury cars and absolutely no one of substance to share it with. Don't get me wrong. There were always women around, but they didn't give a flying fuck about me. For many years this was not a bad situation to be in. I knew the game and I also knew how to avoid getting played. Most women never knew where I lived and I had a "no driving my cars" rule that kept them from ever asking. Every once in a while one of them would get past my roadblocks and get into the house and maybe even live with me for a while, but then they would do something stupid, like start moving their relatives in, refer to my house as their house, or tell me after an argument that I had to leave. A few women hemmed me up a bit early on, but I got smart pretty quick.

The funny thing was that when I was ready to settle down I became the relationship X factor. Women wondered why I was so serious all the time. Was I dying soon or—one of my favorites—did I need a beard? The idea of a man choosing to sit you down after a few dates and say that he is interested in marrying soon and having a family and not just fucking made women suspicious and not swoon. In some ways the rejection was good because it removed a lot of damaged sisters from my life, but I was starting to strike out with more frequency.

My light at the end of the tunnel came in the form of a woman shouting, "What the fuck is this?" on the Baltimore Convention Center floor. It was about two years ago when we hosted the annual Home and Garden Fair at the convention center. I oversee event marketing for the facility and I received notice that there was an exhibitor causing a scene on the floor. Apparently the event organizers could not calm her down and our security couldn't control her either. The floor manager said that the woman was belligerent and telling all of them to "go fuck themselves the hard way." You could not miss the fracas. A group of about ten people were standing around pleading for the woman to just step off the floor and into a side office, and there in the middle of it all was a woman telling them, "Hell no. All I needed was the hookup that I was promised."

You could not miss the sister either. She was head and shoulders above the crowd—definitely over six feet tall—and she had her long braids piled into a huge bun on the back of her head. Her arms were going and her lips too, trying to get the group to simply see her point: that she would not be ignored in some office, and all she needed was what she had been promised.

I approached the group ready for battle. I had my usual weapons. First off I would ask her what was wrong. Then I would apologize for the issue even if it wasn't the center's fault. I would then attempt to resolve the issue. If she still was unhappy, I would refund her exhibit fee and ask her to leave the floor. The final step was to call the police and have them take her out. Most people were just happy to get their money back. For some reason I had the feeling this one would be more difficult because when I walked up and one of the event reps introduced me as the convention center manager, the woman turned, looked me dead in the eye, and said, "What is his corny suspender-wearing ass going to do? Call the police? Even their asses could not get me out of here today." This was going to be harder than I'd thought.

I told Volatile Lady that I was really there to help. I told her my name was David Voorhies and I wanted to make sure that she was happy with her exhibit experience. The Home and Garden Fair floor management team had started to talk about how she hadn't paid for an electric hookup and how there were no booths currently available with electric when I saw the lady lose it again and just throw one of the plants from her display down on the ground in disgust.

"They just don't fucking listen," she said. "They just keep talking." It was then that I identified the issue. This woman did not like being managed, and this group was trying to manage away her problem. I told them to go back to work. Smarty, the security guard, looked at me as if to say, *Are you sure?* before he finally walked away. Once they were gone the lady calmed down enough to finally tell me what was wrong. She was an interior designer and she had forgotten to sign up for booth space with electricity. She had a friend a few booths down with electricity that she wasn't using and she didn't mind swapping out the space. The show had not started yet and she just needed the okay to switch spaces. "I didn't want any of them to do a thing other than just say it was okay, and they all get up in my face not even listening to what I have to say. By the way, my name is Deja," she said.

Seeing her calm down, I said to her, "Deja is a beautiful name. Look, I am sorry that none of them was able to give you what you need, but I am more than willing in the next twenty minutes, before the doors open, to help you get your things down to the other end. You and your friend are going to work out how to explain to people what happened because all of the convention maps will now have you listed incorrectly, but if you both don't mind, then the center is cool with it." She didn't answer and went behind her table and started packing up, and like I'd promised, I helped her wheel her boxes down to her new space.

Hours later I was walking the exhibit floor when I came across Deja doing her thing. She had four women demonstrating to a group of about twenty how easy it was to create faux finishes on walls. Her conversational style and simple delivery made the crowd feel that they could run home and turn their walls into marble. She was a home improvement tutor. She could do it all, from basic carpentry to custom painting. Her forms for in-home demonstrations were disappearing fast. I waited for her demo crowd to thin out before I got closer and asked her how things were going. Deja said, "Much better than this morning, and by the way, thanks for your help."

"No problem. I was just doing my job."

She laughed and said, "You need to teach a few others how to do theirs better."

Deja walked me through her business model and told me that this was just something that she'd loved to do for years, and when she retired from the post office she'd decided to do it for others and get paid. Her business had grown fast. She was even redesigning the Tulley's chain of restaurants. She'd met the wife of the owner here the previous year and was hoping that she'd pick up another big fish this year. Deja handed me her card and told me that if I ever needed a woman's touch around the house to give her a call.

"Why are you so sure that I don't already have a woman in my house?"

"Judging by the snowman suspenders you're wearing, either you don't have a woman or you have one who obviously doesn't care." Her bet was that I lived alone and had "walls screaming to be rescued from paneling."

The truth was I did, and I took her card knowing that I would call.

I called Deja a few days later and scheduled a time for her to come by and check out my place. That Saturday morning I tried my best to clean up the house. The cleaning lady had been off all week, and I hadn't really cleaned up after myself for a few years. I ran around the house with a dust rag and the vacuum and lit a few candles. Until I remembered what she did for a living—I was that carried away by her energy, to tell the truth—I figured Deja probably wouldn't even notice the condition of the house. Most women are just blown away by its size. I have a five-bedroom home on a four-acre lot. The media room seats ten, and I have a backyard pool with an outdoor kitchen and waterfall. Further back in the yard there is a basketball court. I purchased this home from a former Ravens wide receiver who had a contract in Baltimore and then after the championship season went on to bigger things. This house wasn't a big deal to him, but it is the entire world to me. My family makes fun of me living in a family house with no family. And even I must admit that at times it is just a little too quiet. I do use the pool, but I like to watch and not play sports, so the court has been dormant for years. In spite of all that, I still just love the wow factor of my home and hope one day not to feel so lonely in it.

I was out front sweeping off my steps when I heard a car screech to a stop in the driveway. Deja was behind the wheel of her BMW 745i with the windows down and a CD blaring. She hopped out of the car and grabbed her work bag. "Cute house," she said, and whizzed past me through the doors. I knew this "consultation" was going to be live. I watched as Deja went from room to room. She was definitely as tall as I remembered and had the carriage and confidence of a woman who might have modeled when she was young. Deja was a naturally pretty woman who wrapped her God-given beauty in fabulousness. Nothing about her was dainty, soft, or remotely subtle: big hair, long nails, bright clothes, and biting wit. She struck me as a woman raised in a family of brothers or who had worked for years around men. Deja said what she thought and did not back down. My kitchen was "okay," my bedroom "needed a lot of work," but my media room was "incredible" (I know). Her main point of displeasure was that many of the rooms had no definition. Deja told me that I should fix up the gym area and convert one of the five bedrooms to a reading room, adding, "You could stand to do a push-up and read a good book." She had me laughing from the time she came in, and when she finally sat down after our mad dash around the house, she declared my house "not as bad as I thought it would be."

Deja pulled out a pad from her bag and started noting items

that she'd be able to help me with: new carpeting, painting, room restaging, and decluttering. I was impressed with her ability to decipher what my needs were, ask for the business, and then close the sale. I told her to run with creating the gym and reading room and once that was done I'd consider carpets and custom paint in the rest of the house. Deja shook my hand and told me that she would get some prices to me by Wednesday of the next week and that if I could hook her up with some of my neighbors she'd be even more flexible on her pricing. I told her that I would keep that in mind, but not to be too stiff on what she gave me the next week. She laughed and headed toward the door. Once outside on the porch Deja turned to me and asked, "You are a curmudgeon, aren't you?"

"What?" I said.

"That has to be the reason why you can have so much to offer and still be alone. You must be hard to live with. Not that there is anything wrong with that, because I'm a little stuck in my ways and forever single too."

"So we're in the same boat," I said.

"Not really," said Deja. "At this point in your life you still want the dream. Women can smell it on you almost like desperation. I am different. We are probably the same age, but I am okay with being single because I'm not alone. I have plenty of friends, family, and godchildren. You seem a little isolated to me, here with all the things that good women are supposed to want, but none of them seem to."

There was an uneasy silence between us, Deja clearly feeling like she might have said too much and me thinking that maybe she was right on point. "Look," she said, "I apologize if I said too much. You should know by now that I kind of go with the moment, and right then I felt that I was supposed to say that to you. I hope we can still do business, and if another message weighs heavily on me, I promise I will put it in an email *after* the job is done. Deal?"

"Deal." I watched her as she drove away, wondering if Deja was here to do more than fix my house.

• • •

Oh my God, when is this woman leaving? I thought. For the last three days there had been nothing but people stripping my walls and carpets and nonstop banging. There were all kinds of deliveries and returns and the most annoying high-decibel laughing that I just could not get away from. Deja and I had settled on a price for the two-room redesign and she'd been all business since arriving on Wednesday morning. I'd taken a few vacation days to keep an eye on everything, but I was starting to think I would have been better off going into work.

True to her word, she and her crew were in at eight to speak to me and then were off working until five. I never saw them, but I heard them everywhere. In between building bookcases and installing floors I heard, "Girl, no he didn't," or "She said what to you?" The talking never stopped. I thought if I went up and checked on the work they would slow down the talking and pick up the work pace, but when I went upstairs they were knocking the work out. By late Thursday the gym only needed its equipment, and by Friday morning Deja was already asking me about my preferences on what books I wanted to keep and what new books to order for the reading room. She hadn't lied: they were going to be in and out, and I would love the end result. What I'd seen so far was fantastic.

Friday came and went and I still had not gone through my books, as Deja had requested. Saturday morning the fitness company was assembling the machines in the gym, and instead of running upstairs with them Deja came down to the basement to find me. "Is there a problem with the books?" she said.

"No."

"Voo, they don't seem to be making the long trip from floor to bookcase. I can put them in my way, but I really want the room to work for you. We can knock this out in ten minutes, just you and me, looking at what you have and coming up with a plan. Give me ten minutes from online poker and I will change your life." There she went again, calling me "Voo." She'd started calling me that to irritate me when I didn't follow her instructions. It drove me nuts, but I have to admit, I found it kind of funny. I placed the laptop on the coffee table and stomped up the stairs. I did not want to think about books at all, just winning my online poker game so that I could recoup a few of the dollars I'd spent on redecorating.

My new reading room had fabric-covered walls, deep mahogany bookcases, two leather recliners, and recessed lighting. Deja had knocked this one out of the park. Right in the middle of the elegance was my collection of well-read thrillers and history books. Now that I looked at the torn covers, bent pages, discolored images, and water-stained bindings, I wasn't sure if these were even bookcase-worthy. "Maybe it's best to just toss them. Most of them look a little worn out," I said.

Deja was on the floor sorting through the books. "If I were you, I wouldn't throw them out. You obviously enjoyed these books, and keeping them around will remind you of that. All we have to do is smack glass doors on those shelves and every title will look top-notch."

I sat across from her and started stacking up the classics and my favorite mysteries. Deja was working on biographies and all my books on ocean life and boating. I was working so hard on my pile that I hadn't noticed that Deja had gotten really quiet. When I looked up she was leafing through a coffee-table book of the world's finest yachts. I asked her if she liked boats and she said that she did but had never really been on one. Her dad used to make miniature boats, but they were too poor to have one of their own, so they would always tour the boats docked at local ports. She said Norfolk was her favorite because the whole town seemed crazy for all things nautical. I went through the piles and found other books that I thought she'd enjoy: one with historical boats and another with images of the *Queen Mary*. Deja soaked up the info and really seemed interested in something that had been my passion for years. "Do you have a boat?" she asked.

"No, I haven't really gotten around to that one. I don't know why. Just not too motivated, I guess. Maybe I prefer the pretty pictures."

Deja rolled her eyes at me and said, "If you love them so much, you should have your own. I am big on getting what you want out of life."

"Is there anything in Deja Wallace's life that is a letdown or are you really just a go-getter all the time? We regular unfulfilled and goal-challenged folks want to know."

Deja pinched my arm. "No, I haven't always had what I wanted, but you learn to celebrate what you have, and often things really turn around without you doing a thing."

I think I fell for her on the floor of my new reading room. While sorting through my mess of old college textbooks and cookbooks that had never been cracked, Deja told me her story. She was the child of one of those couples who were together forever and just never married. Her parents had met at a party and were inseparable for the next fifty years. They never felt the need to make it official, and somehow it kept them in love. Superstition kept them from doing the deed even at the thirty-year mark, when their four children came together and asked them to. Deja's parents always said they didn't marry because then they could never divorce.

Deja was the youngest, and her parents were pretty old when she was born. Her dad had worked full- and part-time jobs to get the others at least through community college, but when it was time for her to go to school her parents were in their late sixties, so she knew that she'd have to find her own way. She went from high school straight to a postal job and found that she loved working a route. Deja enjoyed getting to know people and interacting with them in the streets. She was happy with the choice she'd made.

Fifteen years into her career at the post office she received her first breast cancer diagnosis. It was not a total surprise because her mom had passed away a few years before from the same disease. The tumor was removed, and she went through the whole dance of chemotherapy. Deja was off her route for nearly a year and a half. When she was ready to return to work they had given her route to someone else, so they gave her a position in quality control at the main office to get her sea legs back. She was bored to tears and yearned to get back on the street, but when the other breast developed cancerous cells, Deja had to make some hard choices. The cancer treatments had pretty much killed her chances of having a child because of the exposure of her eggs to the chemotherapy. She was thirty-five at the time and had to make peace with never being a mom. She'd probably get assigned to another back-office position at the post office because she'd been out so much. Those last two months at home while she was recovering served as a time to really look at what she was doing in life—coasting, not wanting or really expecting more than what was given. It was then that she decided to start living her life.

Deja left the post office and did nothing for six months but use television redecorating shows to make improvements to her house. When the shows no longer fed her desire she went to the home improvement stores for classes. She noticed that the male instructors made things hard to understand and definitely had no patience with a woman looking to learn to install plumbing, tile, and the like. Deja saw that there was room for a woman who could teach both the easy stuff and the large projects too. That's how Diva Destinations was born. She started with a few family members and former co-workers as clients, and soon her referral pool was out of control. Deja took a good idea and turned it into a passion that far exceeded anything she could have accomplished at the post office.

That night I discovered that there was far more to Deja than I ever could have imagined, and I was hungry to learn more.

On the day the reading room was finally done, Deja saw to it that her team cleaned up and was paid. She hung around a few extra minutes to walk the site with me and make sure that I was happy with the improvements. The work was top-notch. I wrote Deja a check for her work and walked her to the door. She turned to me and said, "Voo, take care of yourself and this lovely house. Don't mind me and my jokes. Your Miss Perfect is still out there."

I looked at Deja directly and said, "Yeah, I think she's out there, but I don't think she's checking for me."

"Why would you say that?" said Deja.

Right in that moment my mind was saying, *She is setting you up to ask her out!* I could have easily stepped out of my comfort zone and asked her out for coffee on Sunday or even asked her to stay for dinner. I wanted to spend more time with Deja, but I was scared that she was too much for me. She had the maturity that says, *I have seen it all and you can't fool me.* Anything I attempted with Deja had to be correct and in order or she'd call me on it. I wasn't sure if I was ready for this. But on the other hand I was tired of playing games and really just wanted to be with someone and have it be easy and aboveboard, and that was what being with Deja would be about. She stood in the doorway looking for me to take the step. I saw it in her eyes—*Boy, ask my ass out. You know you want to*—but I didn't.

I said something crazy, like "She is probably in the clubs or still living with her parents"—a totally stupid answer, trying to get Deja out of the house before I poured myself into her the way I wanted to. Deja laughed at my stupid-ass answer and shook my hand. I told her that I would pass her cards around at work. She thanked me and stepped outside. On the way to her car I watched how confidently she strode away from me. Her body was long and solid. Deja was not unsure of her effect on a man, but she knew that there was far more to enjoy in life than just saying that you had a man. I'd had my chance to say I was interested and I'd blown it. She was not going to give me another one. Deja threw her bags in the trunk of her car and headed over to the driver's side to get in. She waved at me one last time, winked, and hopped into the car. That was my chance at a real relationship, and I let it go because I was too scared to be a real partner to a real woman.

As soon as I closed the door, I was on my cell looking through my phone book for a little hottie to call up. I needed to prove to myself that living the high life (money, women, trips, and luxury cars) could be far more fun than getting real with someone (sharing, caring, encouraging, and growing). Maybe I was wrong to want to settle down. I might not be cut out for it. Who needed a real relationship when I could have as many hookups as I could stand? There was nothing lonely or needy about my life. I could have it all whenever I wanted and when I decided that I was ready to.

I hit 7 on my cell phone, for Angel Sanchez B-D. Angel was someone I'd met about two months ago when I was on a blind date from hell with someone else. I spotted Angel at the bar with her girlfriends. As soon as my date got up to use the restroom, I had the waiter drop my business card and a drink off to Angel. Angel was exotically beautiful, with golden brown hair down to her waist, and was the perfect petite package. She had on the highest red heels I'd ever seen. While my date went on and on about the pain of getting over her ex (no man wants to hear that!), I was staring at Angel crossing her legs and flexing her feet in those shoes on the bar stool right beside her. My date eventually caught on, and after calling me an asshole she left. Moments later Angel came to sit down. We didn't really talk all that much that night, but we danced and after about half an hour of Angel backing that ass up on me we were all over each other in my truck. The sex was fast and okay, but we had not hooked up since. Tonight I needed a reunion and a guaranteed fix.

Angel answered, and after a few not-so-subtle moments of her trying to remember who the hell I was, she finally said, "You drive the yellow Hummer." She could not remember my name or riding the hell out of my dick—just my truck. Angel asked me where I lived and said she'd love to come by. An hour and two martinis later Angel was ass up in my living room totally naked. Before she arrived I'd been trying to remember why I had placed "B-D" after her name in my phone. Right now I remembered exactly. Angel was Catholic and saving vaginal sex for marriage. Her specialty was anal sex, and lots of it—B-D stood for "back door." Angel was in front of me with one finger in her pussy and another in her butt. She was working both fingers inside of her and moaning. She was doing so well on her own that she might even have forgotten that I was there. Angel had arrived earlier at my house with only two requests: that I make her something to eat and that we be done by ten because she was meeting her girls at a club downtown and it was only free for ladies until eleven. She was what I needed, right? A young woman to screw my brains out and make Deja go away. Deja would not be ass up finger-fucking herself in my living room if she were here right now; she'd be asking me about my favorite cartoons as a child and what my first job was. Deja probably didn't travel with her own vibrating butt plug and digital camera to capture the memories for her Facebook page. My mind was drifting away from a scene that men would pay for and toward a woman who was far more stimulating. I was trying to hang in there with Angel. I had taken my dick out and was rubbing to the pace of her finger-fucking herself. I let her lick my balls while she played with her toy. Hell, I'd even titty-fucked her and snapped pictures because she thought that was "freaky as hell." I fucked Angel up the ass just to get her off and out of my house, but that did not work because she wanted to see me cum. She wrapped her mouth around my dick, but I wasn't getting there. She was doing her best, but I just was not feeling it. I looked down and saw a young girl who thought that her ability to ass-fuck would make a man marry her. She probably thought she could ass-fuck her way into my truck, my house, my bank account, and maybe even my heart. As her mouth twisted around my dick I felt sad for her because she didn't see how flawed that was, and no one would probably ever tell her that this shit was called getting off, not finding love. She could give the best blow job of my life tonight and I would still not call her back, speak to her in the street, or introduce her to my friends. We shared nothing and she meant nothing, and I would forget about her after this night the same way I'd forgotten about her two months earlier and the same way I'd forgotten so many others—because there was nothing there. It was sick and twisted, but right when my dick exploded in Angel's mouth it became clear to me that I needed her to go and Deja to come back.

I went through the motions with Angel. Held her exactly for two minutes and rushed her into the shower. We stood there in my oversized shower while I washed her body off and she went on and on about how much fun she was going to have at the club later that night and how she thought she might be able to hook up with an Orioles player at the club because that's where they came after the games. I'd just gotten through fucking her and she'd just sucked me off and there she was standing in my shower while I was washing her back telling me that she was looking to fuck a bigger and richer dude later that night. It was official: Angel was a dumb-ass. Once we got out of the shower I told her that I had to get up early for a flight the next day and that I'd call her when I got back. She dressed and left with a quick peck.

Deja did not answer her phone, either cell or home. I tried her cell again to just leave a message to call me back, but this time she actually picked up. "Hello, David. Is everything okay?" Deja said. Her tone was all business, and I was David again—no longer Voo. The intimacy from earlier that day was totally gone. Deja was making her point loud and clear: I'd made the choice to keep it business, and she was not going to take it any other way. There was a lot of laughter in the background, and Deja was whispering into the phone. It did not even occur to me that she would be out on a date. I was really playing myself by blowing up her phone.

"No, um, everything is fine," I said. "Just wanted to ask you something, but it sounds like you are busy, so I'll call you some other time."

"David, I'm going to step outside and call you right back." Deja hung up before I could tell her not to worry about it. During that minute of waiting for her return call, I thought of what I was going to say. That I'd never had that much fun just being around a woman in a very long time. That Deja removed my usual indifference and made me feel like I needed to court her for her attentions. That I felt old-school when I was with her, like I should be making her a mix tape, picking her favorite flowers, or beating up her enemies. I wanted to be her man, and that was the scariest thing for a man to admit—that I thought I might have met the one.

My phone finally rang back, and Deja told me that she was in D.C. at the Improv with some of her friends and that she couldn't really talk in the club. She wanted to know if something had gone wrong with the house. I quickly told her that the house was fine and that everything was working fine. She got quiet as she waited for me to continue. I couldn't speak. I lost all words. I was back at my front door earlier that day watching her wave and drive away, wanting and needing to say everything, but scared of giving away too much. "David, what's up? You gonna get my ass jacked out here by myself in front of the club," said Deja.

"Um, I was wondering if you'd like to maybe have breakfast with me in the morning. I totally understand if you don't, but I'd really like you to." The phone went silent.

"David, I know you didn't interrupt me getting my laugh on for an IHOP invitation. What do you really want? What is it that you want to say?" Damn, Deja was right. I was trying to mack her with some lame-ass invite for pancakes and eggs.

"Okay, let me do this again. Deja, I just want a chance to get to know you a little more and if you have some time tomorrow, I'd like to see you."

Deja laughed and said, "You are finally ready to graduate from the minor to the major league. Those twentysomethings are wearing your wanting-to-be-settled ass out. What happened tonight?" I knew she'd see through me, and she did. I rambled on and on about feeling bad about the way I'd handled things earlier in the day and just needing to see her one more time. Deja must have thought I was high, because she tried to calm me down and assure me that I'd see her tomorrow. "I don't know if you are drunk or traumatized right now, David. I will be at your house first thing in the morning. I have got to go back in, but call me if you need to talk." She hung up the phone, and I knew that I'd freaked her out. She would probably never speak to me again, fearing that I was some chronic drunk dialer or crazy stalker. I went to bed certain I'd fucked up an opportunity again.

My doorbell rang at five in the morning. I shuffled from my bedroom to the front door thinking it was the paper man again with another reminder about the bill. No matter what I did, I could not remember to pay that little-ass bill every three months. I knew my paper man a little too well, and he was one hell of a collector. I opened the door with my latest excuse on the tip of my tongue when I saw Deja still dressed from her night out with coffee and donuts in hand. I'd forgotten how sexy she was outside of those overalls and bandannas that she'd worn the whole time she was working on the house. I invited her in, and she followed me into the kitchen. Instead of stopping at the counter she went out to the deck. I pulled my robe tightly around me and followed her through the French doors. We settled on the chaises, and Deja handed me a cup of coffee and a glazed donut. She said she'd made certain the coffee was black because she wasn't sure what it would take to get me back to my senses after my rambling earlier. She was here if I needed to talk, or she could just sit here and clear her head from the night that she'd had, which probably had been just as crazy as mine.

I sat for a few minutes taking the scene in. Deja had come to see about me because she cared. She'd brought me something to eat. This was a woman doing something for me because she wanted to and not because I might be able to do something for her down the road. She wanted to be here. I was amazed; that *never* happened.

Deja told me about her night. How she'd thought she was going out with some friends to see a local comic and it turned into a matchmaking session with her girl's newly single cousin in town for the weekend from Atlanta. She could not believe her girl thought she'd be interested in this dude; he was short and timid, and he had no sense of humor. He laughed at none of the jokes that night. My call had actually given her an excuse to get out of there—"Because my friend needs me," she'd told them. It had taken her another hour to find a place open with fresh breakfast goods, so I'd better spit some important info to make up for her bad night.

We were sitting there watching the sun break through the clouds, and it was an incredible sight to see. I had lived in this house for years and never thought to just step outside and see this. I was not living my life. It took Deja to take me outside to show me—it was time to live. I sipped my coffee and opened up to her.

I told her about Angel and how I'd felt nothing for her and how lonely I'd been feeling for months. I told her how I felt like a failure because nothing carried any weight or importance for me, and how I feared I was destined to be the old man in the club, the one who dies alone because he is too selfish to share his life with someone else. The very last thing I told Deja was the most important—I felt weight with her, importance with her, and a connection with her, and I wanted to find out where the journey would take me.

I was anxious for her response. It was as if I had just handed her a note asking if she liked me or not and she was tapping her pencil looking as if she might write in *maybe*. I just stared down into my coffee and waited. This was worth it. We sat silently while the squirrels jumped from tree to tree. Deja placed her hand on top of mine and moved in closer to me. She placed her free hand on my cheek, pulled my head to her, kissed me softly on the cheek, and said, "It's going to be one hell of a journey if we do this, Voo." I was more than up to meeting Deja's challenge.

Belinda

> My mind needs to be blown. I am tired of failed promises and mis-steps in the dark. I need to be turned out. Make sex real again. Make me scream your name. TS098

Sex is so disappointing. So many promises and far too little action. Most men like to talk about their big dicks, oral skills, and back-blowing abilities, only to hit for a few minutes and then fall asleep. Few, if any, know what a female's orgasm looks like, and fewer still can tell you how to make one happen. And often brothers are the worst because they seem to brag on their stuff so much it's almost impossible to ever back up all the talk. I've had some whoppers over the years:

- Curtis, the barber, who always came in my face when I expressly told him to let me know and pull out.

- Marcellus, the dancer, who could not have sex unless the lights were on and there was a mirror close by. We hooked up because I loved his body, and the truth was he loved his body too.

- Brandon, the bus driver, who could tell you how to get anywhere in the city in ten minutes but who could not for the life of him find the right hole. He stuck it in my ass "by accident" so many times that I began to think that was his hole of choice.

But the award went to:

- Celin. He was a great lover. He knew all the right things to touch and was romantic and interesting, but he also liked me to yell out strange things in the middle of sex, like "Smack me, slap me, bite me." I had no problem saying these things and even letting him get a few licks in, but one night he drew blood and would not stop and I knew that it was time for him to go. A few weeks later he jumped me at my front door and forced me into my apartment. I maced his ass, thinking I was getting mugged. When the cops came he said he was my boyfriend and that it was only foreplay. I told them to lock his ski-mask-wearing ass up for assault.

See, men don't get it. There is value in meeting someone, being intrigued by him, and having a mutually satisfying sexual experience. It has been a long time since someone made me want to call him in the middle of the night to come over, and even longer since someone made me want to be monogamous. The last guy who did it all for me was my ex-husband, Busby.

Busby was the full package—smart, funny, gorgeous, and sexy as hell. We met at my family reunion. I will never forget walking into the welcome mixer and seeing him standing there. He was just a few inches taller than me and built to perfection. His abs, arms, and chest were barely contained by his tee, and he had the largest calves I had ever seen. This was a man who worked out for a living. His skin was the color of a ripe peach, and he had a curly ponytail at the base of his neck. I could not stop looking at him. I was staring so intently that my sister had to snap me out of it by saying, "Belinda, he's probably a cousin . . . stop staring." Damn, she was right.

As much as I tried, I could not stop checking for Busby. Later that night at the pool, I saw my dream man walk into the pool area with what looked like his mom and sister. They lounged on the chairs and seemed very comfortable with one another. Instead of torturing myself further, I decided to jump in and cool off. I did a few quick laps to clear my head and resurfaced. The two women also got into the water, leaving the dream guy solo on his lounge chair. I got out of the pool, and he watched me walk from the pool's edge all the way over to my chair. *Yeah, get a good look. I know you like what you see,* I thought. But okay, this was twisted; it was time to clear my mind.

As I dried myself off, I heard a voice from behind say hi. I turned to see that it was my dream guy. I managed a quick hi before turning my back once again on him. He said his name was Cory, but that everyone called him by his last name, Busby. I told him that my name was Belinda, and I asked him whose family branch he was part of; I told him that I was one of the Whatleys. Busby quickly corrected me. "I'm not a member of your family. Trust me, I am not into dating my cousins." I laughed and told him that I thought it was a little strange that he was trying to get hooked up at a family reunion—his or anybody else's. He explained that he was a soccer player, originally from Panama, studying at Georgetown. His roommate was kin to me, one of the Donnellys and he'd just joined them on their annual trip to the reunion; he pointed to his roommate's mother and sister, who were still wading in the pool. Busby had a few months left until school finished, and he was going to go pro. So he wasn't a cousin, and I could not have been happier. From that moment on Busby and I were together.

Busby and I dated for a year. I was in my senior year at American University when he went pro and asked me to marry him. My parents went ballistic when I told them that not only was I getting married at twenty-one but I was also dropping out of school. Busby was going to be traveling a great deal and I wanted to be there with him at every game. We were going to Vegas to get married in a few weeks and after a quick Hawaiian honeymoon we were hitting the road with his team. My mom cried for a week and my dad would not even look at Busby when he came over to the house. They liked him, but they felt that he was wrecking the plans that they had for their youngest daughter. I understood how they felt, but when you want to be with someone you simply do not care.

A week before we were all going to fly out to Vegas, Busby came by our house and told everyone to get in the truck; he wanted to show us all something. My mom had softened her opinion of our situation, not wanting to be so mean that she got left out of the planning, and my dad begrudgingly came along just to not be the last one to see the surprise. After about a half hour on the road Busby pulled down a long brick driveway. At the end of the driveway was my house. I knew immediately because I had taken Busby into this subdivision often, saying that this was where I'd always wanted to live. The house was in a gated community in Potomac right off of the golf course. It was yellow stucco and huge. When he parked the truck my parents bolted from the back and I just smiled at him. This was much too much house for two people, but I saw this house for what it really was—our start— and I was happy. Busby excitedly led me from room to room as the sunlight danced on my skin. Each room was larger than the next, and the kitchen and bathrooms were designer dreams. When we finally got to the master suite, Busby lifted me up and carried me over the threshold. I told him that you were supposed to do that after you were married, but he didn't care; this moment was just too special to pass up. Right there on the floor of the room were three business cards. Each card was for a different decorator. Busby told me that I could interview them all and order whatever I wanted. This was my house, and I was to make it as special as I made him feel. I hugged him so tightly. No one had ever gone out of his way for me like this. This man loved me, and all he wanted in return was my full attention and devotion.

I finally made my way back downstairs after checking out all of the upstairs rooms, and Busby said that I'd forgotten to check one of the rooms out. I told him that I hadn't missed anything—I'd been all over that house making plans and staking out my own private areas. The only place I had not been was the garage, and I already knew what a garage looked like—an empty room. When I told Busby this, he simply winked at me. With that I ran to the other side of the house, through the kitchen, and into the garage. There in one of the four spaces was a brand-new Mercedes SL roadster. It was burgundy—my favorite color. The tags said BUS-BLDY. He told me that if I did not want it he could take it back. I looked at him like he'd lost his mind. A Mercedes beat my 2005 Sentra any day. While I sat in the garage in my brand-new car, too scared to even really take it down the driveway, Busby snuck in the house and gave my parents the keys to the Range Rover. He told them that we would hang out at the house for a while and that he would bring me and my new Benz home in a few hours. My mom knew what was up and just shook her head disapprovingly, but my dad forgot all parental responsibility, grabbed the keys to the Range Rover, and hopped in to get his full mack on. The Whatleys were getting comfortable being the in-laws of a professional soccer player.

Standing in our living room looking out of the windows onto our front yard, I could not stop shaking my head. Busby asked me if I was okay, and I told him that in fact I wasn't. This was all so much more than I ever expected, and I could just cry from all the excitement I was feeling and the gratefulness I wanted to show. I told him about how lucky I was that he loved me and how hard I was going to work to support him in all that he would do. I was so happy in that moment, and I needed more than anything for him to get that.

Busby turned me toward him and told me that he understood how I felt. He was so excited about the future and finally having things in order. I had made him a better man—he had someone else depending on him, so he could not squander his opportunities or his potential. He loved me, and more than anything he wanted me to know that that one fact would never change. Busby pulled me close to him, lifted me up, and wrapped my legs around his waist. This was always his favorite thing to do because he loved the fact that I was so small and he could easily bend me the way that he needed me. I locked my legs behind his back and I thrust my tongue into the secret areas of his mouth where he was most sweet and warm. I ran my hands all over his face. His skin was buttery smooth and the cologne that he wore filled my nose and started to play with my mind. I ran my hands along the back of Busby's neck and removed the rubber band from his hair. I loved playing in his hair. Long hair on a man was new to me; I loved the way it felt on my skin and my lips, and the smell was always intoxicating.

Busby began to place me on the floor but suddenly changed his mind. "Let's try something different," he said, and with that he grabbed my hand and ran with me through the house and up the stairs to the master suite. Once we were in, he led me into the bathroom and turned on our own private steam shower. He was right—there had been quite a few sexy baths in our past, but definitely no sauna. Busby came over to me and stood before me doing his little striptease. Look, there is no shame in my game. Busby is a professional athlete who's paid to eat well and exercise—his body was no joke. He had muscles all over and abs that defied reason. He had no tats to break up the hard, chiseled yellow tone of him that I loved so much. Our routine was that he would always strip for me to get my visual going and then I would take the next step in our kinky dance.

Busby slowly removed my T-shirt with his teeth. He grabbed the hem at my waist and ran his mouth up my torso and over my exposed breasts. I was almost always braless, a perk of having small firm boobs that drove him crazy. Then Busby went behind me and crouched down, using his teeth again to inch my skirt down around my thighs. Unfortunately, my panties came down too; I was aching for him to attack them with his teeth as well. I stepped out of my flip-flops and followed him into the heat of the shower. There as the fine gray mist surrounded us our bodies locked together—curve against curve and sweat intermingling. I loved the harmony of our skin tones next to each other, my fine premium chocolate against his butterscotch coating. I was definitely one of the sistas that was color-struck, but I long ago got over other people's perceptions because I simply want what I want.

Busby ran his hands all over my body and began to push my shoulders down, angling me to my knees. It was my turn to take the lead, and I was the lead when it came to giving head. First I sucked Busby's balls. I took each of them in my mouth, coating them with me, and then gently rocking them back and forth until it was time to give his thick shaft all of my attention. Busby was incredibly thick. His dick was a welcome visitor to my mouth. I made it feel at home and at peace. My tongue ran laps around his tip while my hands tickled his shaft, making him mumble that I needed to go faster because he was about to bust. While I was working on his dick Busby was running his fingers through my hair. I kept a fabulous short cut, but the heat of the shower made my blowout pointless, and now I had curls all over. This turned Busby on because he liked it best when my hair was curly. His fingers were working my scalp, directing my head where he needed me most. I took every inch of him into my mouth, popping him in and out so that he could hear my lips smacking and know that I was enjoying it. My head was going faster and faster and deeper and deeper into Busby's pelvis; he wanted as much of my mouth on him as possible. Just when I thought that the ramming was uncontrollable his warmth oozed into my mouth. I swallowed all of it and even licked off the bits that rolled down his cock and balls. Another benefit of dating a man who handles his health is that he tastes extraordinary. Busby always tasted great, probably because of all the those protein shakes that he inhaled all day long. I loved pleasing him this way, and Busby loved letting me do it.

I got up off my knees and Busby sat on the bench in the steam room. I lay across his lap ass up and waited for my special treat. His left hand hit my ass with a force that I was not ready for. The first blow was always the most shocking and pleasureful. Today he wanted to be rough with me, and I was up for it. Busby's hand was sending fire up my ass cheeks and down my back. My pussy was contracting from the excitement and I felt myself growing wet. He was whacking my ass fast today, making sure that he left a little sting in between. When my body tensed up on his lap from the tremors he knew that I was ready. Busby sat me up and placed me on his lap facing him. He then grabbed my waist and hoisted my legs up onto his shoulders. I mashed my pussy into his face while his tongue looked for my wettest spot. Busby was a clit man, and he played it like a master, licking and blowing on it until it swelled into submission. I knew that it was coming and I pushed Busby's head back so he could see. Right then my body shook and a white liquid, my love liquid, shot out of my pussy. Busby opened his mouth to receive it all. He kissed my pussy like it was a precious child and brought me down onto his lap. Busby looked at me and said, "I can't wait until you are my wife so that I can finally know what you really feel like inside." Yeah, Busby and I did a lot of nasty things together, but we were saving going all the way until marriage. Sex with him was always going to be an adventure.

Busby and I were married one week later, and everything about our lives was fulfilling. I finally experienced his cock inside of me, and it was yummy. The house was being decorated in fine style, and there appeared to be a cease-fire with my parents. Being married to Busby was wonderful. I followed the team during the season, and when he was not playing we traveled all around the world. He had no reservations about spoiling me. We eventually filled that big house with art and gifts from everywhere. Our house was family central with its huge yard, pool, and media room. It took about five years for us to finally get to the point where we needed more than just the two of us. Cory was such a blessing, and we basked in his perfection. Busby, Cory and I were the perfect family package, and I could not imagine any other life.

Soon, like most new moms, my time became absorbed by everything Cory. My days were filled with feedings, play groups, and tiny tot activities. It was hard for me to travel as much with Busby during the season, and when Busby was home, I had to split time between him and the baby. At this, my man, who was so used to being the center of everything, began to distance himself. First there was less just me-and-him time. Then there was less sex. The final strain was having little to even talk about. He loved his son but was not real concerned about the latest play group gossip. I still followed the success of his team, but I started to view the world of sports as a small part of my life. There were greater things about our world than a goal.

Honestly, this went on for months and I barely noticed the slow slide. I was too busy to notice that Busby rarely spent his off-season nights at home or that he had little time or patience for my indulgences. My mom stayed with us for a while to help out and suggested that I go on a weekend trip with my husband for some one-on-one time away from the house. Our little trip was not the best because all I could think about was whether or not Cory was okay and when we would get back to him. It was as if the obsession that I once had for my husband automatically shut off for him and turned on for my son. In my head, I thought this was what Busby would want—me making sure that the home ran smoothly—but after a year of distance Busby came home and told me that in fact this was not what he wanted and he was moving out.

I love hard and Busby did not want to share that love. He is a definitive decision maker, and he chose to move on. I knew to not question the decision. Our game was always played on his terms, and this was going to be the last play.

So Busby and I have been divorced for the last five years. He was fair to me in the divorce settlement. I got to keep the house and the cars, and the alimony and child support more than cover my expenses. The first year of the divorce was difficult because there was still a lot of love there. There were times when I wanted to ask him to work it out, but I knew he would not have left if there was a chance for us to smooth things over. Eventually we have come to a place where we are friendly. I can be around him and not think of his lips on me or the way his hair smells. Busby no longer watches me pull away when I drop Cory off at his house. We greet each other as old friends who share a great passion—our son. Surprisingly, the divorce brought Busby much closer to his child. I think when Busby felt that he no longer had to compete with Cory for attention and affection, it was easier for him to love him as a son.

Busby bought a house a few blocks away and we alternate weeks. Cory, now a robust six-year-old who is all boy, basks in his dad's attention and loves sports with the same focus as Busby. The biggest change has been that Busby has remarried. Veronica was Busby's manager when he decided to retire three years ago, and she's been the driving force in repackaging him for endorsements and coaching gigs. She is about ten years older than Busby, can't have kids, has a great stake in Busby's career success, and is crazy about my son. When I first found out they were dating I thought I'd be jealous, but I surprised even myself by becoming cool with Veronica. The thing is, if she keeps Busby happy, he stays successful. And if he is successful, my household stays successful, so in my mind she better work it out!

But of course there is debris in my life—fallout, if you will. Yes, my financials are tight, my kid is thriving, and overall I am pretty satisfied with my strides over the last five years: completing school, running a little bakery, and getting my finance groove on to protect Cory's future. But I have not been able to exactly get my groove back when it comes to sex. Sometimes I wonder if I should just make the great compromise that so many friends have made: sleep with guys that are simply "good enough." But honestly, I think I'm too spoiled for middle-of-the-road anything.

. . .

I continue to be heavily invested in Cory's success. With his growing attraction to sports, I am now familiar with the intricacies of the game, whatever game it is. Usually Busby handles getting him signed up and outfitted for his teams. It has always worked out great because the local coaches geek over meeting Busby, and so our son sees prime positions and lots of playing time, while other kids whose dads are not quite as famous have to play the luck game. This week, though, Busby is out of town at a conference and it is Mom's job to get Cory out to the field for his first practice. As usual, Cory is so excited that his focus is off. After several trips in and out of the house for socks, cleats, and water, we finally set off.

Once at the field it is now time to search down Coach Richardson. I've only spoken to him briefly on the phone, and he told me that he would have on red shorts and a cap. Who knew that it was going to be red shorts and cap day at Royal Field? There are at least four other men with clipboards running around in that outfit. Shit. These are the times when I really wish Busby could just handle all the sports stuff. Cory goes off to run around with some of his friends from school, and all of his equipment is getting pretty heavy on my shoulder. Just when I think I am about to lose it someone in red shorts walks over to me. "Mrs. Busby?" he asks.

"Ms. Busby," I correct him. "You must be Coach Richardson," I say. "I have never been happier to see a man dressed in red."

He laughs and takes the equipment from me and places it on the ground. "Which of these guys is Cory?"

I point to the shortest runner with the biggest mouth. "He's quick . . . a good thing for us," he says.

"Yeah. I only hope that you can channel all of that energy so that I can have a knocked-out kid in about two hours." Look at me! I am flirting and loving every second. Coach Richardson chuckles and walks with me to collect Cory, telling me the proper way to dress Cory for playing and how this is all about teaching them the fundamentals and getting them ready for competitive play down the road. Cory is going to be fine and have a lot of fun in the process.

I am an awful mom because while I do watch Cory warm up and do drills, I am way more intrigued by Coach Richardson. He looks to be in his midthirties and extremely athletic. He is a tall guy, probably about six-four, and light, the way I like them. The thing most striking about the coach is his goatee: it is a wild mix of gray and black, almost exotic. It is thick on his chin and on the sides of his lips and shaved clean above his lips, and I cannot help wondering about how it might feel going down my belly, circling my neck, or brushing against my toes. I want to touch it, it is that beautiful.

At the end of practice Cory runs over to me and Coach Richardson follows. He lets me know that Cory did well and that he looks forward to working with him. I thank him and stick out my hand to shake his. There is no ring, but years with an athlete taught me that this really means nothing. He could still be married and not sport his ring during practice. Oh well. We will have to see.

Even though I've been a bit nervous that Busby will catch on to the source of my interest at the field, I still go with them to practice and all the games—so what if sports is supposed to be the boys' thing? Coach Richardson is *my* thing. Some days Busby gives me his typical "something's up" look, but soon lets it go to tell me about his latest sports initiative. I've forgotten how much Busby loves talking about himself—a really good guy with an incredible sense of self. Veronica—God bless her.

Coach Richardson is always so patient with the boys. They listen intently to him and he really seems comfortable with the chaos of coaching young boys who'd rather run around chasing one another than block, tackle, or throw. Busby has forgotten all about me and is only into making sure all of the other parents know who his boy is. I let him have his fun while I play out all sorts of fantasy scenarios with Coach Richardson in my head. Coach Richardson blowing his whistle at me to switch positions. Coach Richardson spanking me with his clipboard. Coach Richardson pouring Gatorade all over my body and mopping it up with his goatee. I told you it's been a while since I had it good!

At the end of one game both Busby and I walk down to collect Cory. Coach Richardson walks over, and Busby being Busby, he jumps in to claim his territory as Cory's dad. Coach Richardson says it's a pleasure to meet Cory Busby Sr. and that he liked both his college and professional play. At that Busby lights up like Sunday morning and offers his expertise if they ever need a fill-in coach because he was a decent football player in high school. Coach Richardson thanks him for the offer, shakes Busby's hand, and turns to walk away. Just when I think that unfortunately he, like so many men, is awed by Busby's star power, he turns and says, "Ms. Busby, good to see you again . . . don't make it the last time." All I can do is smile and nod, and with that Coach Richardson runs off to the next family. Busby turns to me and before I can put my smile away he once again gives me the "gotcha" eyebrow and shepherds Cory and me off to the truck for the ride home.

Over the next few weeks my brief conversations with Coach Richardson at the end of games mature from Cory's progress to what we did during the day (he's a project manager), city versus country life (he lives on Capitol Hill), and great places to eat when you are alone (he is definitely single, and we discover we both found at least one good spot in the pages of *TEASE*).

All of the conversations have been polite and not too over the top. We are walking the fine line of keeping things professional while maintaining an undercurrent of "We cannot wait for this season to be over." This was about my son's football future and not about his mom getting some. And Busby's stopped looking at me like I'm crazy when I join him and Cory for practice. He can tell what's going on, but like a typical guy he chooses to never talk about or think about it. Honestly, I believe Busby does not want to think of me with another guy until he absolutely has to—like when I am married. We still ride to most practices and games together and Cory seems oblivious to Mommy's covert plan.

The last game of the season our team wins. It's taken all season for our guys to pull it together and run in the right direction. Cory is crazy excited and he clings to Coach Richardson's hip as they leave the field—that is, until he sees Busby and shoots like a rocket into his arms. Coach Richardson approaches us and thanks us once again for our support throughout the season. Busby thanks the coach for his hard work and with Cory wrapped around his shoulders works his way through the throng of kids and parents toward the truck. When I turn from Busby and Cory back to Coach Richardson, he's standing just looking at me. I am at a loss for words. I lock my fingers around my bag to stop them from springing up to touch his face—or worse, to cop a feel. "Thanks for being so good with Cory," I say.

"My pleasure. He is a really talented kid. Get ready for another pro in the family," says Coach Richardson.

"Well, Coach, I guess we will see each other next year."

"We'll see each other this Friday night at about eight at a restaurant of your picking, Ms. Busby. And by the way, my name is Melvin."

I blush while he jots his cell number onto my hand. It is so grade-school, but it is the most enticing moment I've had in a long time. The stroke of the ballpoint tip on my hand makes me wonder about other "balls" and "tips."

Friday night, I am too nervous. There have been many dates since Busby and I split, but for some reason I feel like I have to get this one right from the beginning. We've agreed to meet up at Clyde's in Chevy Chase for drinks and a quick meal. I've known Melvin casually for months, but this is going to be the real test to see if there is really something there. I decide to go with my Rock and Republic jeans, some heels, a little white tee, and of course the

Rolex. There's no need to hide it. I am a high-end girl who deserves the best, and Melvin needs to see my value. I am upstairs trying to get my lashes in the right spot when I hear the bell. I wait a second to hear the lock turn, realizing it's Busby coming to pick up Cory. We both had keys to each other's house, but after Busby remarried I volunteered to give my copy of his key back. I wasn't seeing anybody seriously, so I had no problem with Busby being able to just come in. Maybe after tonight B will have to give up the key.

Usually Busby merely yells to me from downstairs that they're off, but tonight I hear him climb the stairs heading toward Cory's bedroom. He must have forgotten a toy or picture that he wanted to show his dad. On the way back downstairs, I hear Busby tap on my bedroom door to say bye. I guess I don't respond quickly enough, because he comes right in. "You okay?" he asks.

"Fine!" I yell back. "Just trying to get my face on." He rounds the corner by the bathroom door and stops when he sees me. He rubs his lips with his hand and smiles.

"You look good, Belinda. Have fun tonight." And with that he waves and scoops Cory up in the hallway, and I hear the front door shut behind them. We get weird rarely, and I thank God above that we are both mature enough to know that we were pretty important to each other at one time and that because we may lock eyes once a year that does not mean that we screw up our arrangement. Just by saying that I look good Busby eased my tension over the night. It's moments like this when I know that Busby and I did have something special. It wasn't meant to be a forever thing, but it was real.

I pull up to Clyde's at eight and have the valet do his thing. Inside the restaurant it's pretty dark, so I just make my way to the bar and order a ginger ale. I learned a long time ago that drinking really isn't for me, especially in social situations. There is no buzz for Belinda, just falling-down drunk, which is never sexy. At about 8:10 I decide that I'll leave in five minutes if Melvin doesn't show up. Wow, to go through all of this anticipation for nothing. It would be a bit surprising, but not at all shocking. When the clock behind the bar reads 8:15, I reach into my bag to pay my tab. It's then that I feel a hand on my back and hear Melvin's voice, apologizing for being late. He sees my credit card in hand and takes it away from me. "I got this," he said. He throws a $50 bill on the bar for my $7 drink and takes me by the hand out of the restaurant.

"What are you doing?" I ask.

"Are you in the mood for an adventure?" he asks, directing me toward his car, which is parked out front. He makes sure I'm in and quickly jumps into the driver's side. In the car he again apologizes for being late, and says that at the last minute he thought of a way to really make the night memorable and he just had to do it. "Don't bother asking me questions, because I'm not going to answer any. Just relax and enjoy the music, and we'll be at our destination in a few minutes." Melvin places his free hand over mine, and I settle into the leather seat, close my eyes, and relax.

A few minutes later I open my eyes as the car stops. I barely recognize where we are because it is so dark. Melvin grabs a duffel bag from his trunk and then takes my hand to lead me into the darkness. He must notice my "Are you going to cut me up and scatter my body parts?" face because he quickly says, "It's going to be okay."

He leads me down the narrow path toward the football field. He hands me the duffel bag and runs over to the small field office to turn on the field's lights. It's quite beautiful. I feel as if I am in one of those sports movies where the lights are so blinding and the grass is almost Technicolor green. Melvin removes his jacket and places it on the grass at my feet. He pulls me up toward him and says, "It is only proper that our special night be at the place that we first met."

Now, typically I would say this is a cheap-ass trying to hide his cheapness with creativity, but oddly enough his statement makes me feel warm inside and I think it's actually kind of cute. Melvin could have pulled a box of Fig Newtons and a Sprite with two straws out of that bag and I would still be there.

He directs me to sit on his jacket, and he opens his bag of treats. Inside he has all of my favorites from Carolina Kitchen. "I cannot believe you remembered that!" I told him that was my favorite place to eat when I was feeling alone. He then pulls out the biggest bottle ever of Canada Dry ginger ale, because I told him how much I feel like a kid when I go out because I don't drink. The final item that he pulls from the bag is a small DVD player. He hits play and on comes an episode from season two of *Soul Food*—my favorite show of all time. "This is so thoughtful and creative, Melvin. Thank you." But then I realize something: "Hey, what's here for you tonight?"

"You."

We sit out there for hours, just eating and talking. Melvin tells me that he almost got married once but really wasn't ready, and since then, even though he's dated many women, woefully few have been able to hold his attention for more than one night. "I still like innocence in women, a sense of play and a positive spirit," he says. "But I am not into the twenty-five-and-under set, and most women who are older are too hurt to be happy."

"Why do you feel I'm any different?"

Melvin looks me in the eyes and says, "From that first day, I saw in you a woman who didn't take herself too seriously, liked to have fun, and was generous to her child. I was a little worried when I found you had an ex, but seeing you guys together, it became pretty clear that you two were handling things well and, more importantly, that it was all about Cory. Busby didn't pull any man-up stuff with me at the games, and that's how I knew he wouldn't be an issue. Do you know how bad I wanted this season to be over just so I could get to know you better? And this is our most winning season ever! But you know what, Belinda? Tonight, you're proving I was right. You are the chillest woman I've been with in quite some time."

It is my turn to open up, and I give Melvin the quick version of Busby and me, that we will always be in each other's lives but we know our boundaries. I let Melvin in on the fact that most men are either intimidated by Busby and the things that I have as a re-sult of our marriage or by the fact that I need a lot when it comes to relationships. I tell him that I realized a few months ago that I am always on a mission to be connected and am finding most men don't even know what that means. For once I'm being honest with a man about my need to be filled mentally, emotionally, and sexu-ally. "And until that can happen," I tell him, "I would rather just be alone."

Melvin's listening intently, and with each nod of affirmation he's demonstrating that he has a soft side, isn't intimidated by my circumstances, and seems to be looking for quality—all things that have been problems for other men. I tell him that I am very interested in seeing where this would go.

We finish eating and I gather up our trash, putting everything back into the duffel. Look, I am a girl—and horny, at that—so of course I'm on all fours in front of Melvin with my ass poked up in the air so that he can check out the merchandise. Once everything is put away, I lean back on Melvin for a minute just to look up at the sky. Melvin puts his arm around me and starts stroking the bare skin of my arm. He asks if I'm cold (goose bumps!) and moves me onto his lap, holding me even more completely. I feel him run his nose along the base of my neck and the edges of my hair; the thickness of his goatee against my skin is everything that I imagined that first day. I stand and sit back down on his lap, now facing him. I can hear his ears calling my lips to come closer, and I take up the call, kissing and licking them. My tongue wants to taste his lips; who am I to deprive it? He tastes of almonds, and it's setting my body on fire.

In between my legs I feel Melvin's growing excitement. I pull away from him. "We can go back to my house," I say.

"No, I'd rather stay here. I've always had a thing for playing fields."

Me too.

Melvin pulls my tank top off and then removes his shirt. We lie for a long time chest to chest, making out with the desperation of teens afraid that they will get caught and may never again get the chance. I kiss Melvin down his chest and belly and pull his pants down around his waist. His dick is one of the most beautiful I've ever seen: so straight, strong, and willing. I have only started to lick the tip when he pulls me up to face him. Melvin takes my jeans off and rubs his hands all over my body. I inch my hips up—hungrily—to meet his, but he is not making a move to insert himself; instead, Melvin rolls me over onto my back. He says, "Belinda, I don't like to rush. We have all night and I really want to experience you. I am not into a sex-by-numbers type of situation." He kisses me some more while his dick bounces against my thigh. I am going insane and have to tell him how much I want all of him inside of me. I whisper in his ear, "Please put it in me . . . please put it in me."

"Not yet," he answers. "There is a little something that I need you to do for me first."

Melvin flips over onto his stomach and directs me to lie belly down on his back. He pulls my face next to his and, barely able to catch his breath, says, "I need you to bite me . . . my ass . . . my shoulders . . . anywhere, and I will give you anything you want."

I ease my face down to his hard, round ass and take a bite. Spreading his legs, I bite his entire ass and slip a few licks in on his balls and the tip of his dick, which is now swollen and peeking out from underneath him. Most women would be freaked out by Melvin's request, but I am so turned on. As he gets up, ready to slip on a condom and take me completely, I reflect back on the ad I have pending for *TEASE*. Could my curse of sad-sex men finally be broken? My next pro is definitely ready to play.

Destiny

Must Lock Doors

Crave a dark, wet, and warm space where I can grow and release all my tension. Are you my place? Highly qualified Peter looking for a new Paula. TS555

'd been so hot for Denae! But he'd been dodging my calls for weeks. This brother felt no need to call me after our night together. Four weeks of resentment had built up to the point where I never wanted to talk to him again, much less sleep with him again. He played me, plain and simple. Denae swooped in with all of his sexy and his flash and I was powerless to resist. I would not be that dumb again.

But then he smiled.

I came in from lunch and there he was on the couch in the reception area. He smiled at me and my pussy twitched. We went into my office and he told me how busy he'd been the last few weeks. While he was talking, I thought about what it would be like to ride him on my desk. Denae knew he was having an effect on me, and he would lick his lips and smile; my resolve was growing weaker by the minute. He told me that he missed me and that he couldn't get our night together off of his mind. (*Yeah, right,* I thought. *You should have called.*)

Denae popped up out of his seat saying that he had to go but that he would pick me up after work. I looked at him and told him that I had plans, and he looked right back at me and told me to change them. Then he hugged me and gave me a small bite on the neck. My skin was on fire from that little bit of contact and I knew that I could definitely get hotter. My head said to leave Denae alone, but my pussy won this argument, and I was sitting in Denae's car at five o'clock.

As soon as I got in his car he leaned over and kissed me on my cheek. I said to hell with being polite and I turned his face to mine for a full-on kiss. I had been fantasizing about him for weeks, and I wanted this more than anything. Denae pulled back and said, "Damn, girl, slow down."

I couldn't and I didn't. I placed Denae's hand on my thigh and told him that I didn't want to grab dinner. I told him to go to my house because I wanted him to myself. Denae turned the Mercedes around and headed toward my house. Once inside we literally tore each other's clothes off and just fell on the cold wood floor of my living room as warmth spread between my legs. Denae's head was buried deeply in between them; he was hungry and doing as much as he could to please me. He came up and thrust his dick inside me. The force of his body pounding into mine and the way he whispered how much he'd missed me made my eyes well up because I wanted him so bad, but I knew that he would be gone as soon as this was over.

Denae touched everything inside me as I screamed his name. He rolled me over onto my stomach and entered me from behind. He was pulling my hair and pushing himself even deeper inside when I heard my door bust open and a female voice cry, "What the fuck?"

Denae jumped up off me and I flipped over onto my back and drew my legs up to my chest. There in my living room were the two plastic women from the club that night. One was up front and center yelling at Denae about how could he do this and what type of fool did he think she was? The other chick was by the door and seemed to be there to have her girlfriend's back. Our dumb asses had been so hot that we'd forgotten to lock the door behind us, and Denae's "girl of six months," as she quickly informed me, had followed us back to my house from the office. *Is this really happening?* I felt like I was back in high school being tortured by the cool girls. I grabbed a blanket from the couch to watch it all play out. It was like watching Maury Povich's show up close and personal. Denae was stumbling around, trying to get his clothes on and explaining how "this chick"—me—"does not mean anything" to him. The pissed girlfriend was going on and on about how he kept doing this silly-ass shit and she couldn't believe that she stayed with him. I sat quietly on the couch waiting for them to just get the hell out of my house. Between the embarrassment of being caught with another girl's man's dick in me and listening to him go on and on about how I was nothing, my ego could not sink any lower.

· · ·

The final stages of our "segment" played out like this:

- Pissed Girl hits Denae all up in the head with her Coach bag and tells him that she should get someone to beat his ass and maybe then he'd respect her.

- The girlfriend of Pissed Girl is all up in my doorway daring anybody to leave the house before she says it's time.

- Denae is apologizing up and down to Pissed Girl. He turns his back to me and says to her that this was a moment of weakness and that she shouldn't be jealous because Pissed Girl was the hottest woman he'd ever seen. (A few minutes ago my pussy was the best he'd ever had. I guess things change.)

- Me: *Negroes, please just leave so that I can curl up in my bed and have a good cry over how stupid I truly am.*

Eventually they all left, with Pissed Girl following closely behind Denae's Benz with her matching Benz. They were probably going back to his place to have makeup sex and laugh at how pathetic I was, just sitting there letting them wreak havoc in my living room. I was a joke in their world because they were meant for each other—drama and lies go together, and there was no room for common sense or any other form of normal. I had done what I said I would never do again—I let good dick rule over my good common sense, and Denae was the winner all around.

The following day I walked around the office in a state of disbelief. Things like that just do not happen to women like me. I am smart, right? Worldly, right? Not desperate—well, maybe a little desperate, and that was why this fool had been able to get in. . . . My phone rang, and it was Deanna notifying me that there was a package for me at the front desk. It was a small Tiffany box. Deanna said Denae had dropped it off. I took the box back to my office and opened it. Inside was a sterling silver Tiffany key ring with my initials engraved on the back. The note card contained a single word: *Sorry.* Denae's ass was sorry, and I threw the package in the trash can.

I'm done with trying to convert bad boys. It's time to switch up my game.

I turned my computer on and pulled up my latest emails filled with pinky fuckers, penis rings, and lube lovers.

At least my freaks were clear on what they wanted.

Lilly

High-maintenance chick looking for her next benefactor. Wants the best and can give the best. Only men who are already what they aspire to be need to reply. TS6235

I have been divorced for six months now and I am still having a hard time accepting it all. When I first divorced I dreamed of being free. All the men I would date. The places I would travel. The sheer freedom of just doing what the hell I wanted when I wanted. But since the papers were signed, all I have done is go to work, come home, go to sleep, and start it all over again the next day. I am too wrapped up in small details to really move forward. Things constantly throw wrenches in my "you are no longer Mrs. Dellum" game plan. The other day I was putting my summer clothes away and came across my wedding album. I sat on the floor of my closet for an hour poring over the pictures and well wishes, trying to figure out how you could spend eight years with someone and never ever again be as happy as you were on that first day. Telemarketers nearly send me over the edge calling to solicit Mrs. Dellum, and when I tell them that it is now Ms. Wyse I secretly wonder when I will stop getting these little reminders.

My family has been attempting to be supportive, but I am just not as ready to move on as I thought I would be at this point. Last Saturday my mom wanted to have a girls' night out with me, and we went to the movies; I was a bawling mess about forty-five minutes in, when the couple decided to call it quits. I am talking inconsolable crying, where eventually I had to leave the theater to get myself together. After the movie my mom tried her best to encourage me to stop thinking about Frank and move on, but I just was not up for the whole "Frank was an ass" conversation. I love my family to death and I am so thankful for their support, but the truth was that my marriage was far more complicated than your typical "guy has done you wrong" scenario.

I was Mrs. Frank Dellum for eight years, and it was a crazy mix of great (wife of a highly successful entrepreneur) and not-so-great (constant lies, stress, and worry). Frank was the owner of four of the city's hottest gentlemen's clubs. His brand, Lilac Lounge, was tremendously popular because it was a strip club that successfully married traditional nightclub, restaurant, meeting space, and dancers all in one facility. Everything was upscale and aboveboard. There were no under-the-table sex, drugs, or money deals in his establishments. He wanted Lilac to be a destination and a place to meet all of your entertainment needs. Our strippers were real dancers with perfect bodies: no tattoos, stretch marks, scars, or anything else to take away from the fantasy experience. When you walked in there was a massive set of stairs that would take you to the various levels of the lounge where all of the clientele mixed and mingled. You came dressed to impress or you could not get in, which made it hard to distinguish between strip club clients, tourists in for a great dinner, and hip-hop heads looking to sample the latest underground artist. When I met Frank he had only two Lilac Lounge locations, and after we were married we worked together to open Lilac 3 and Lilac 4. We were a great mix of friends, lovers, and business partners, and I believed there was no way that we could lose.

• • •

At the start of our relationship I was a media manager for the mayor's office and we were looking to book space at Lilac for a community development celebration. One of the business owners being heralded at the event was Frank. I know it seems odd to honor your local strip club owner, but Frank's dedication to going into developing areas of the city and breathing new life into them, creating jobs with decent salaries, and single-handedly reviving the old burlesque club vibe made him a bit of a local celebrity. Plus when you own the best entertainment venue in a city you see a lot of things, and powerful people in the city knew that keeping Frank happy would in the end keep all of them happy and off the front pages.

I didn't really think all that much about my meeting with the owner of Lilac. Me and my girls had been there a few times—it was the spot for bridal parties on Sock Night, when the men came out to do their thing onstage. I thought the place was pretty fun and the service was always excellent, so I was really just looking forward to a great lunch and getting the contract negotiated.

Once I walked in I was greeted by the hostess, who placed me in the private elevator to Frank's suite on the top floor of Lilac 2. There I was greeted by the most beautiful dark chocolate man I'd ever seen. His skin was the color of dark-roasted coffee beans. Frank was well over six feet, with the thickness of a man who might have played college football back in the day. His suit hugged his body, and all his jewelry, from his Cartier watch to his platinum bracelet, seemed to catch the sunlight. He was far more attractive, refined, and polished than I'd expected. I took so much time taking him in that I was actually caught off guard when he extended his hand and introduced himself.

We had lunch and discussed the event at a small conference table in his office. Frank was all business, making sure he understood what we needed that night and also what his business was going to get out of the deal. Not once during the whole two hours we were together did he even allude to the fact that I was attractive or even a woman. It was weird for me because most men acknowledge an attractive woman even if only subtly, staring just a little too long or asking questions in an attempt to figure out if you have a man. Frank did none of these things; he talked to me about his business and his plans for the future, asked me about the inner workings of the mayor's office, and pretty much stayed all business all the time with me. When his assistant came to the door with the final event contract in hand, Frank handed me the envelope and walked me to the door. As I stepped on the elevator, he placed his hand inside the door and simply said, "It was a pleasure to meet you, Ms. Wyse, and if you ever want to take in dinner and a show, just let me know and I will make it happen."

After a week of going back and forth with my girls over whether or not that was a come-on, I finally broke down and went to Lilac for dinner with my girl Natasha. Natasha was the Man Whisperer. If a guy was even remotely interested, she could see it in his walk, his aura, and all types of other crazy stuff. Once we gave our order to the waitress I asked, "Is Mr. Dellum around? I am Lilly Wyse with the mayor's office, and he asked me to let him know when I visited." The waitress said she would check to see if he was in. Natasha was about twenty minutes deep into her latest work dilemma when I felt a hand squeeze my shoulder. I looked up and there was Frank smiling from ear to ear.

"Ms. Wyse, great to see you again . . . Are you enjoying yourself?" asked Frank.

"Please, call me Lilly. And most definitely, everything is wonderful as usual," I replied. Natasha kicked me under the table. "Oh, this is my friend Natasha," and Natasha reached out and shook Frank's hand.

"Well, ladies, enjoy your dinner and let me know if you need anything. And Lilly, is it okay if I give you a call next week?"

"Please do," I quickly replied.

As he walked away Natasha said, "He's interested. He's just a lot smoother than the average brother." Then she excitedly pointed to the small table that Frank had settled down at. "Lilly, is that Frisco White and his brother Marc over there?"

"I guess so. Kind of strange for them to be out having dinner with the city police all over their asses," I replied. The White brothers had been rumored drug dealers for years, but they were able to hide most connections through their legitimate front as bail bondsmen. Bodies had been dropping around the Whites for years, but they were geniuses at having others take the fall. "Isn't *TEASE* doing a special series on them this week?"

Natasha bobbed her head, excited to be sitting so close to one of the hottest stories in Baltimore. "Yep, I read the first part during lunch today. You won't believe all the people they think the Whites may have their fingers on."

Tonight for me was not about the White brothers or city gossip or political goings-on. I just looked at Frank and raised my eyebrows slightly. He grabbed his wineglass and toasted me. I smiled the smile of a girl being noticed by the most powerful man in the room and allowed myself to bask in the glow.

The rest of the night we sat back in the luxurious booth and watched Frank Dellum work his magic on his customers. They all loved him and they all wanted just a few seconds of his time to confirm that they were part of his world.

I awoke on Monday to the incessant buzzing of my BlackBerry. Who was calling at six in the morning? My office knew that talking to me before my Starbucks was an impossibility, and my mom knew that if someone wasn't on fire or under a bus, she should not dare to call until after nine. I slapped my hand on the phone and flipped it over, and with one eye open saw "Frank Dellum" pop up on the caller ID.

"Hellooo?" I breathed heavily into the phone, trying to gather my thoughts.

"Hey, Lilly. I hope it's not too early. It's Frank Dellum from Lilac. I wanted to catch you before you got to work," he said hurriedly. "Look, I want you to have dinner with me at the club tonight around nine. It is going to be a fantastic meal and drinks, and I think you'll like the crowd. I will send my driver for you at about eight-thirty."

Frank was not one to ask. He assumed that no one could turn down an invitation from him, and he kind of bulldozed the pleasantries usually associated with asking a girl out. Dellum was business even when he wasn't doing business. Having dinner with him was either on my mind or not. Frank was not going to entice me. He was just going to have me.

"Frank, it is so early, but I'd be a fool to turn down a free meal. Can I bring a friend?" I threw that in just to show him that it was not going to be as easy as he thought to lock me down. I knew he was asking me out on a date, but a girl always has to appear to have other plans.

There was a short silence, and then I heard Frank take a deep breath and laugh a little under his breath. "Lilly, you can have as many guests at dinner as you want, just not tonight. I want to sort of be the center of your attention."

I threw the sheet over my head and rolled onto my side, cradling the phone to my ear. At that moment I could care less about the cancer risks of jamming your cell phone to your ear. I wanted to hear all of Frank's reactions and imagine the warmth of his voice.

"Well, in that case, no friends, and I will meet your driver at eight-thirty. He can pick me up from the mayor's office downtown. We have a council meeting tonight." I tried to sound calm and unaffected, but I think my excitement was showing through. As weird as it may sound, I think I could hear Frank's smile through the phone. Our "thing" was starting tonight, and we both could not wait.

The council meeting couldn't end fast enough. When the gavel dropped, I ran up to my office and grabbed my heels and makeup bag from my desk. In the ladies' room I attempted to make the transition from day to night that all of the makeover shows say is so easy. The day had been insane and there was no time to sneak home for a fresh outfit, so I'd have to make do with what I had on all day. I stepped back from the mirror and was pleased with what I saw. At thirty I was fit and fabulous. I had a body that was small enough to be considered petite but curvy enough to be considered all woman. My saving grace was a tiny waist and great legs that made me look pretty good in just about anything. Most people thought I was attractive, with skin the color of oak and long dark hair. The hair was Remy's finest, but since I'd had a weave for years most people thought it was mine. While some thought my weave said "I am ashamed of my blackness," I knew it said, "I pay $1,500 every three months to look perfect every day."

With a final shake of the hair and retouch of my lip gloss I was down the stairs and into the warm leather seats of Frank's Maybach heading toward Lilac. Once I arrived, I was escorted up to Frank's office, and to my surprise behind the curtains in his office was a balcony dressed with a table for two with fresh flowers, candles, champagne, and chocolates. I hadn't known that Lilac had a balcony, and it was a beautiful summer night in Baltimore. The city hummed with sirens and chatter beneath me, but the view of the skyline was breathtaking—the lights, the moon, and the few stars were captivating. I dropped my suit jacket and bag near one of the chairs and let the light summer breeze run along my back. I was so thankful that I had worn the halter dress suit to work that day because without my jacket the dress fit me like a glove and was cut perfectly to show off my smooth and toned back. I held on to the railing and with one hand pulled all of my hair over one shoulder to the front so that I could get a bit more air on my shoulders and neck. I had that feeling that this was going to be a night that I would never forget, and it had not even officially started yet.

Just as I started to wonder where Frank was, I felt the light touch of a finger on my lower back.

"Now what is this?" said Frank. I felt him circling my small tattoo of a star. I sometimes forgot that it was there. Definitely the tattoo had been a peer pressure move as a freshman at college. Everyone else was getting their man's name tattooed on their breast, tribal tats on their arms, or some sort of Asian scribe. I was both scared and broke, so I played it safe with a dime-sized star in a spot that my parents would probably never see. Somehow this tattoo along with the heat of Frank's fingertip tracing it felt like the perfect match.

"You like the sky, I see," said Frank. He came in closer, wrapped his arms around my waist, and brought his head down to my left ear. Generally I would be offended that someone got so close without being invited to do so, but with Frank it felt natural to be encircled cocoon-like in his arms. His chest was massive, and his arms were thick and strong. I felt secure with him. I leaned my head back a little and gave him the perfect vantage point down the front of my dress. He peeked but quickly took his glance from my breasts to the skyline in front of us and said, "You know, this is the start of us."

I turned around and looked Frank directly in the eyes. Without moving back he grabbed the railing behind me, one arm on either side of me, and said, "This is the start of us, and you are not leaving this room without being mine. I knew it the moment you walked in my office." Frank continued, "I see it this way: you have been playing with boys, and now I want to show you how a man closes the deal. I think you're game, but I will give you an out if you are not ready for this."

With that Frank removed his hands from behind me and folded his arms in front of him. He stepped back and with his skin glistening in the candlelight and his dimples popping, he just smiled and waited for me to give him the go sign. There was never a thought in my mind to leave, but I did have some doubt as to whether I could handle this. Frank was right: I was getting exhausted chasing the up-and-comers and beating back the masses of women going after the select few who weren't even really worth it in the end. I was ready for a mature relationship with a man who was already what he hoped to become and knew exactly what he wanted.

I walked up to Frank and just for fun tried to break left around him. He grabbed me by the waist and brought me closer to him. He smelled of jasmine and cedar. Frank took my face in his hands and made me look up at him. Gently he slid his hands under my arms and lifted me up to meet him face-to-face. He licked my top lip and took a small nibble of my bottom one and said, "I knew you would make the smart choice." As he slid me back down his body to the floor, I felt how turned on he was becoming. His hardness pressed against my belly and all I could think about was what he felt like and tasted like. It was that moment unlike any other when you knew that your thoughts should stop you but your body just wants to move forward.

I looked up at Frank and he leaned in to kiss me. He was an expert at tongue play, sucking me in and releasing me with perfect precision. My hands slid from behind his back down to his sides and then made their way to the front of his pants. I rubbed his cock through his pants, first slowly and gently and then more aggressively. With each stroke his cock grew thicker and longer. He wanted—needed—release, and I wanted to give it to him. I slid down his body to my knees. There with the moon as our companion and the warm city engulfing us, I set Frank free. I unzipped his pants and was surprised to find that he was a no-underwear guy. His cock popped out and smacked me in my nose. Any other time this would have been a "what the fuck" moment, but right then, I wanted him too bad to care. I just scooped him up in both hands and went to work.

Frank's cock was majestic, a full nine inches. My breath was trapped for a moment in my throat as I contemplated whether I could take him in fully, but my mouth watered at its smooth texture and heavy veins pushing to get closer to my lips. I wrapped my lips around the tip, sucking it first, and then I worked my way down to getting his shaft nice and wet. The whole time Frank kept his hands in my hair, positioning my head and mouth right where he needed them to be. I then went to my go-to trick and wrapped my lips around my teeth and made my mouth a playhouse of sensation for Frank, a crazy mixture of wetness, heat, and friction. He was losing it, calling my name over and over again while fingering his balls with one hand and ramming my head into his groin with the other. Just when I thought I was close to blowing his mind he pulled back and turned away from me, cock bobbing in the night air. He went over to the table, grabbed one of the chairs, and placed its back against the railing of the balcony. He came over a few steps to me and retrieved me from the floor, then knelt in front of me, reached under my dress, and pulled my panties off. Frank walked me over to the chair and told me to sit up on the railing and face him with my feet on the seat of the chair. Now, we were several stories up, and one wrong move on the railing would result in a quick introduction to the sidewalk below. I was fearful and intrigued. Could this man pull this off? Had he done this with so many women that this was his mind-blowing go-to? Then I realized that I could either dissect this or get the fuck of my life. "Fuck it!" I whispered under my breath. I hopped up on the railing and faced Frank with my arms locked onto the railing.

Frank removed his suit jacket, unbuttoned his dress shirt, and dropped his pants. As his pants fell away from his body he stood before me with his light blue dress shirt blowing in the wind and nothing else. His upper body was "bumptastic." Huge muscles absolutely everywhere. My right hand crazily sprang from the railing just to touch perfection. Frank stood on the base of the chair and looked me in the eyes.

"You are so damn beautiful, Lilly. I can make you happy. I can please you in ways that no other man can because my shit is real. No lies. No dreams. Just . . . It is what it is, but you have to want it. Do you want it?" Frank whispered in the night air while caressing my face.

"I want it," I whispered back.

"What? I can't hear you," said Frank as he slipped his fingers into my pussy. "I have to know that you want it."

"I want it," I said between quick breaths. With each of my responses Frank added another finger to the mix. When he had three of his fingers exploring my inner walls and a thumb gently rubbing my clit into submission, I finally let go of all of my reservations of what was right and wrong on a first date or what all this might be leading to. I let my head fall back, tightened my grasp on the railing, and yelled at Frank that I wanted it now. "Give it to me now!"

Frank pulled his fingers from inside me and rubbed my sweet love all over his lips. He leaned in and kissed me deeply and we both took in my sweet taste. He stuck his fingers inside me again and leaned back a little as he covered the tip of his cock with my juice. He rubbed himself slowly at first, and then while looking at my pussy he began to stroke harder. When I looked away for a second just to gather all of the sensations of the moment, Frank rubbed himself harder and told me to watch how he liked to be touched.

As he worked his hand up and down his shaft I saw a small bit of Frank's cum slip down the top of his cock. Frank leaned into me and took my arms from the railing. Holding me tightly, he thrust all nine inches into me. I locked my legs around his waist and bounced on his satisfying cock. He was hitting every spot just right, massaging my G-spot from within and grinding with so much force that my clit was about to explode. Frank was a master—twisting me to the right of his body for more friction for him and discovering early on that twisting me to the left set my clit on fire. He pushed himself in me for so long that I knew he was about to come. I had already gotten mine a few times, the first time being when I was giving him head. I was one of those women who definitely got off on pleasing a man orally, and all the excitement generated from him being inside of me was an added bonus. Just as I felt his body shudder a bit, Frank pulled out. I saw his cum spill over the base of the chair, and some went away as droplets in the night air. He grabbed me by the waist and I thought he was going to help me off of the railing, but he simply repositioned me. I grabbed the railing tightly as Frank kicked away the chair.

"Relax, baby, and enjoy this," Frank said. He pushed my legs farther apart and buried his face in between my legs. At first I was guarded, trying to keep myself steady on the balcony railing and not lose all my class due to the party that Frank was maintaining in between my legs. He sucked my clit in and out, and then he started to gently nibble on it. There was no part of my pussy that he missed, especially not once he started alternating between my clit and my hole. The shit started feeling too good, and bravely I removed one hand from the railing to rub Frank's head and bring his face closer to its target. My pussy got so good to Frank that he grabbed my butt cheeks with his hands and brought me even closer. The combination of his tongue making me more wet and his hands gripping my ass and further exposing me to the night air and the street below was driving me insane. Frank had me in his tight grip, and when he moved his hand from my right butt cheek and inserted his index finger into my ass my whole body shook.

I released my other hand from the railing and held on tight to Frank's head. My legs locked onto his head like earmuffs and my body burned and trembled like never before. This was the height that all women seek, and the women who've had it chase the next one like a great new drug. This is what makes women slash tires, act the fool at his workplace, and beat down other chicks. This shit was good as hell and no other guy even came close. Once my body stopped shaking Frank came up for air and helped me down from the railing. Carrying me in his arms, he righted the chair he'd knocked over and sat down in it with me on his lap. Moving my hair away from my face, he kissed me, and all I could do was mutter over and over again, "I want this. I want this. I want this."

We dated for four months, and our wedding day was incredible. I was given a blank check to do whatever I desired because, hey, you only get married once, right? The reception was filled with dignitaries, food, drinks, and the very best entertainment. Frank was my king, and I was his queen. Nothing was ever going to stop us. After our honeymoon in Fiji we came right home and got right to work on Lilac 3. I had quit my job to be a full-time planner for the Lilac locations, and our plans for Lilac 3 were going to have people talking. Lilac 3 would have the same levels as its predecessors, but it would also have a rooftop deck overlooking the city with a huge pool and private cabanas lining the pool for even more privacy. The rooftop would only be for our Lilac Club members and for special parties willing to pay the lofty booking fee. We wanted everybody to know that a party was high-end if it was going on at the rooftop.

Lilac 3 exploded on the scene, and business could not have been better. All the reviews were in, and Lilac and Frank Dellum were a force to be reckoned with when it came to compelling spaces that jump-started development in needy areas of the city. We were on all the right invitee lists; magazines profiled us and our wonderful home. Businesses were literally knocking on our door for partnerships. But as our business relationship grew more and more solid, our personal one was falling away.

The openness we shared early on in our marriage started to close as I noticed more and more people visiting the office during the day that were not your typical businessmen and women. I would enter rooms and conversations would stop. There would be business investors who knew who I was but Frank never told me who they were. And then there were so many young women just hanging around either waiting for their men to finish with Frank or waiting to meet Frank directly. I knew damn well they were not dancers or servers—I knew all of the staff, after all. Things were getting strange around Lilac, and definitely things were out of sync with Frank and me.

My feelings were confirmed when, after a particularly rough audit of our personal and business accounts, Frank revealed to me that the thousands of dollars a month missing from our accounts were going to his two mystery children with two different mystery moms from two previous mystery relationships. Outside of financially taking care of them, he didn't do much else for them, so he told me the "kids aren't really an issue for us."

I was shocked—Frank was so diligent with pills with me because he did not want kids. He'd even gone as far as to make my doctor's appointments for me and check my pill case to make sure I wasn't missing. He was really dedicated to his plan of being married for ten years and building the business before having children. He never told me he'd even had a serious relationship before, let alone kids, but I just let it go because they'd been here before me—really, what could I say? And maybe part of me wasn't surprised, considering that he'd given no thought to contraceptives on our first night—but that was too much to bear. I had it all, and I wasn't really prepared to let go of that fantasy, kids or no.

As more time passed the all-night sex sessions and exotic trips had started to become less frequent. Frank was no longer on pill patrol because six years into the marriage there was little if any sex to protect. For a while I excused our nonexistent sex life because of the stress of expanding the clubs so fast and trying to build our dream home. It didn't matter what I did—Frank was not interested in sexing me. I tried lingerie, nights with our own private dancer, office seduction—none of it worked. My man was not getting turned on, and I was not getting any. When I brought this up to Frank he just waved me off and said that all couples go through this. I believed him for a time until one night I was waiting for him upstairs in the office while he finished saying goodnight to museum benefit guests and he never came upstairs to get me to go home. Two hours passed, and when I had had enough of waiting I went downstairs to look for him. Frank was not in the restaurant or in the private party room with the cleaning staff. I popped up into the strip club level, and he was not in the main room. As I turned to leave the club and return to the office, I looked over to the bar and locked eyes with Colby, our club manager; something in Colby's glance stayed with me. I flipped around to see him heading back to the VIP room and I quickly followed him. Colby was a former intern of Frank's and would do absolutely anything to protect him.

"What's going on, Colby?" I yelled at his back. "Why is your ass running to the back?" He quickened his step, but what Colby didn't know was that there is very little in life faster than a woman on the scent of her man. Within seconds I was on Colby's heels and easily maneuvered around him to hit the door first. The door burst open, and there on the overstuffed banquettes that I'd picked out, bathed in the perfect shade of blue light that it had taken me months to find, were my husband and our lead dancer, Salome. She was straddling Frank's lap and rubbing her fake 42Es while grinding pantyless on his lap. Frank's pants were open and his limp cock was just sitting on his left thigh. It was lifeless.

Salome was saying in her throatiest voice, "Baby, you are so hot. Don't you want to fuck me? Let me lick it and it will be all better." Frank ignored her pleas as he leaned over to the glass drink table on his left, trying desperately with a knife to scoop a white substance into a small pile on the glass tabletop.

I was frozen in the doorway, confused and pissed over what I saw. Colby finally caught up with me and ran smack into my back. In his urgency to protect his mentor he hit me with such force from behind that we both tumbled onto the floor and literally smacked the beautiful oak floors. The sound of us hitting the floor startled Salome, and she hopped off Frank's lap so fast that her knee tilted the drink table up and its contents sprayed across the floor. Frank jumped from the banquette and pushed Salome out of the way.

"Bitch, what were you thinking?" he yelled at her. "What the fuck were you thinking?" he yelled again at no one in particular, like the room had wronged him in some way.

My mind was locked. I'd been all set to walk in and see my man knocking the bottom out of one of our dancers. We had not had sex for months, and he *did* run an "entertainment facility" with the hottest dancers in town. I did not want him to have an affair, but I wasn't stupid; I always knew there was a possibility. This shit, though, I was not ready for—my man, limp dicked, crawling around like a fiend, licking his fingers trying to get coke off the floor of the VIP room. He never looked at me or even inquired why I was there or if I was okay. Nothing mattered to him at that moment other than chasing his high. Things made sense then. Salome was our most talented and beautiful dancer and she could not get him hard. Over the months I had enlisted other dancers for private parties and even threesomes, yet none of these things had gotten Frank off. He always just went down on me or let the dancer of the night get me off. We became toy-only lovers. Frank would use them on me to get me off but nothing made him hard: my lips, the sight of my pussy, me with another woman—nothing. I'd just assumed he was tired of me, but what I'd just seen was that pussy was no longer his lover; white lines were.

Salome grabbed her clothes from the small stage in the room and uttered an "I'm sorry" as she headed back to the dressing room. Colby stood up behind me and then bent over to help me up.

"I didn't want you to find out like this," said Colby. "I wanted to talk to you about it, but didn't know what to really say."

"How long has he been like this?" I asked.

"This bad? Only a few months. It was a hobby for a few years, apparently, but the new stuff on the street grabbed hold of him. He can't shake it." Colby looked down at his shoes as he answered my questions.

"Help me get him up." I went over to Frank. "Frank, baby, it's Lilly. Let Colby get you over to the banquette." Frank looked up at me as if he wasn't exactly sure who I was. Then his look of confusion turned to knowing and he dropped his head as Colby grabbed him from behind and brought him to his feet.

"Wait a second, Colby." Colby stood there with one of Frank's arms around his shoulders as I went down on my knees in front of my husband of six years. He was not the pillar of strength and experience that I'd wanted to take in but a broken man, hooked on coke, who needed me to take control. I pulled Frank's pants up around his waist, zipped him up, and fixed his belt. I looked him in his eyes and said under my breath, "I wanted this. I will fix this."

Colby led Frank out into the heart of Lilac and up to his office to rest. I walked over in the blue light of the room and opened a small closet door. Inside I removed a broom and the fabric cleaner and got to work under the blue lights cleaning up my life.

The very next day Frank began an indefinite sabbatical from the club, and nurses and doctors worked with him around the clock to help him kick his habit. Salome was given a nice severance check in return for her silence, and Colby turned into a real asset, helping me get Frank back on track with perfect discretion. In that time, Frank and I didn't really discuss much. He was my new project, and I was going to fix him. First up was keeping certain folks off our properties. All business came through me, and if you did not have a legitimate interest you did not darken Lilac's doors. All the hangers-on were no longer around, and Frisco White was tops on the list. I'd never liked him, and when Colby hinted that he might have been Frank's dealer I made sure that security kept him away. Colby made staff aware who was running things, and as a reward for his hard work he was now operations manager for all locations.

It took about six weeks for Frank to get back to normal, and by week eight he was back in the office. He looked like old Frank, well dressed, clean, and focused, but when I really looked at him I saw the cracks in the veneer. He was unsure of his place at Lilac because things had been moving so smoothly without him. Instead of acknowledging my and Colby's hard work, Frank simply took what he wanted. What he wanted was control of Lilac back. I was bumped back to event planner and Colby was back in the club. The corporate moves I didn't care about much, but the fact that my man, my husband, would not even discuss his addiction with me or the tumult that it caused hurt more. Whenever I brought it up Frank quickly shut me down with his declarations that he was back and that he'd never fall again.

"Lilly, things are good now. Don't overthink them." My heart sank every time he said this, because Frank's "good" was appearing to be master of Lilac's universe, with his plans for Lilac 5 in Philly and his beautiful wife by his side. The staff had been told there was a small medical issue and that Frank had made a full recovery, and business rolled on. As long as Frank was big man on campus, all was well in his world. It seemed he cared little whether things were well with me. We never discussed Salome, the coke, or the fact that we still had no sex life. We'd tried a few times, but it was fast and unsatisfying. I'd seen behind Frank's mask, and I was not sure if he could be with someone who knew the truth. Frank took to buying me things as his way of showing his love. All his gifts stank of bribery to me, a payoff for not letting him fall totally apart or for not putting his business on the streets. I was lonelier than ever because I was convinced Frank no longer loved me. He had me, but he no longer wanted me. And now there were no drugs to blame.

For many years Frank had been a master at presenting an image of squeaky cleanness, and I'd bought all of it in the beginning. Over time Frank let his guard down and I saw all of the shady lunch deals with politicos and dealers, each lobbying for support. After his big comeback, business as usual crept back into Lilac. I should have known that I could keep our noses clean only so long. The dealers wanted access to rich patrons looking for a fun night in the city, and the politicians wanted to stay in the good graces of Frank and his questionable financial backers. Lilac on the surface was a community dream, but just under the surface it was nothing but another money-laundering organization that facilitated the peaceful and undercover play of the city's elite, both legit and not. Frank was the perfect middleman, clean enough not to be questioned but dirty enough not to be taken advantage of.

But even the strong slip, and Frank slipped hard. One afternoon while in the office I answered the phone. It was a reporter from *TEASE* asking if I wanted to comment on a story coming out in two days about Lilac being linked to the White shootings.

"We have no connections to the White shootings. You must be mistaken," I said.

The reporter pressed on. "Mrs. Dellum, the police have phone conversations and video showing your husband meeting with the White brothers regarding bank deposits and business start-ups funded by the White family's drug sales." I was silent. The room got suddenly warm. "Mrs. Dellum, these recordings were made by Jalisa Bryant . . . are you familiar with Ms. Bryant?"

I sighed. Of course I knew who Jalisa was. She'd been a thorn in my side for years: Frank's ex-girlfriend who would not go away. Frank swore up and down that she was just crazy and there was nothing going on, but a woman does not just hang on to a married man for six years without getting something out of it. Frank had never let me down and I always knew that I came first. Jalisa was just trash, a former dancer at the first Lilac who'd thought since she was dating the boss she could do whatever the hell she wanted. Because she'd been around in the beginning and knew where all the bodies were buried, Frank kept her around, even after he had to publicly fire her for her role in a nasty brawl at the club. He hoped that by keeping her in a nice apartment and a nice car and footing her son's private education that she'd just forget much of what she knew. Apparently not.

While part of me thought that this drug business was his stuff and didn't involve me, I was now co-owner of Lilac Inc., and if what this reporter was saying was true, we were all about to be exposed.

The story hit two days later, and while Frank continued to deny to me that he had anything personal going on with Jalisa, when the attorney general's office reached out to me for my cooperation in the case and showed me the tapes of him in her place undressing her, their calls and text messages of love and sex, and even evidence that Jalisa's son might be Frank's son as well, I started to think seriously about just throwing in the towel on my lying husband. They pressured me hard, because while Jalisa knew a little, I knew more—where the money was coming from and where it went. I could point out who was key to their investigation and who just wanted to play at being a player. I knew the ways the money was channeled and all the creative ways people were paid. Frank had trusted me the most, and if I didn't cooperate, I was going down with him. They gave me a few days to think about it and I was able to finally go home. When I walked into the house it was empty. Frank had been locked up the last two days and the entourage that normally filled our living space had either vanished out of fear or was totally engrossed over at the Lilac offices trying to figure out how to get Frank out. A dutiful wife would have gone straight to the office to work on Frank's release, but there is something about video of your man with another woman hoisted above his head eating her out that makes you think that maybe you shouldn't be totally in his corner.

• • •

Our marriage ended rather quietly. While the press camped outside my door and "no comment" was passed around nonstop by Baltimore's elite, I made the easy decision to save myself. I had kept quiet too long and Frank had taken advantage of my loyalty. I was still young, beautiful, and smart, with no kids, and I could see my way through this. After one day of sulking in the house, I drove myself down to the attorney general's office and told them what they wanted to know. In the end, I got probation for sitting by and not reporting all the secret deals, and I got to keep my piece of our financial pie, the slice that was not connected to the clubs—my very own event-planning business, which I had started two years prior and was doing pretty well with. It took a year for us to go to court. While I was offered witness protection and the option of not testifying in open court, I passed on them both. I wanted Frank to be aware of who had shut him down. Plus I knew much more about city corruption than the AG thought I did, and I made it known on the streets that if I was so much as scraped by accident, all that I was privy to would come to light. I knew Baltimore intimately—good and bad—and I knew that I was safe.

Frank got twenty-five years for money laundering and even more years for his roles in some of the White brothers' killings. Apparently my husband had a side business of hiring ex-cons as shooters—who knew? It took another year to officially divorce and get our assets in order. The last time I visited Frank, right before the divorce was final, he told me how wrong he'd been and that he forgave me for what I'd done. All I could do was smirk and hold the final divorce papers up to the glass.

"I just wanted to see you one last time and to let you know that everything is done," I said. Frank narrowed his eyes as if checking to see if I was serious about this. No need to check. I was definitely serious. He placed his hand on the glass, and for just a moment I was back in his office eight years before, impressed like hell at all he'd accomplished. The dimples were popping and he was the brother with the tightest game I'd ever seen. I placed my hand on the glass on top of his. For a quick second I thought I could hang in there. That I could be there when he got out. That he still loved me. Then it was my turn to search his for real meaning, and all I saw now was a desperate man trying to game me. I removed my hand from the glass, kissed my fingertips and placed them to the glass, then got up and left the visiting room. As tears came rolling down my cheeks, I knew it was finally done, and while it hurt, it was what needed to be done. As I looked down to grab a tissue from my purse I was bumped by someone racing to get to security before visitation was over. When I turned to find out who had just nearly upended me, I saw that it was Jalisa. She was dressed in her prison best, a knockoff Hervé Léger bandage dress and cheap stilettos that clicked when she walked, and she was dragging her son behind her, trying to get to her man before they shut things down for the day. All I could do was shake my head and laugh quietly to myself. Sometimes you get small signs that you are finally on the right path.

Bryce

Sexibitionists, come and get your proper exposure with us. Open group looking for new members and kindred spirits. Safe environment for the adventurous and the curious. TS654

I remember thinking I was quite dull. Even now, I live a pretty simple life consisting of work, church, and family. I wasn't involved in any big scandals, dramas, or controversies. I had no financial problems, baby mamas, hateful exes, or ruinous habits. Each day I clocked in at my job, which pays me decently, and at the end of the day I settled down with my dinner and watched television. I was that man you see every day but never quite notice because there isn't anything particularly special about him: he's not tall or short, not fine or ugly; he may be cute for some and passable to others. I was the nice guy that women write articles and books on and talk about to death on television talk shows.

They say we don't exist but we do. Women are just fooling themselves. They don't really want a *normal* nice guy. They want a nice
guy who looks like Morris Chestnut, slings dick like Mr. Marcus,
lavishes them like a baller, and is a family man like Will. They
want it all at a level that your average nice guy cannot provide.
Thus I was a nice guy fast approaching forty and still single when
I placed this ad in "Hot Sheet":

> Man looking for nothing more than love. I am tired of chasing and
> want a real relationship. I don't care if I sound desperate because
> it's true. I am looking for you. TS345

I never received a single reply, except from the editor, wishing
me luck.

One day I received a page stating that Monica Quints was out
front to meet me. I handle accounts payable at Standard Dodge,
and we had double-charged her credit card for some repairs. I tried
to resolve the issue over the phone, but we ended up playing a long-
running game of telephone tag. Rarely do I see clients face-to-face.
When you deal with collecting money, most people would prefer to
handle it by phone. I quickly grabbed Ms. Quints's file and went
out into the lobby to meet her. She was definitely not the soccer
mom type who typically came into the dealership. Monica was put
together from head to toe and reminded me of the actress Jackeé
back in her 227 days. Curvy everywhere, but still a tight package.
She had a natural beauty touched with a bit of makeup and a lot of
style. She was pleasant and personable while I straightened out her
account. I noticed that her tote bag was from a women's program
at Northrup Baptist. "You attend Northrup?" I asked.

"Eight a.m. every Sunday for the last few years," she responded. "Do you go there?" When I nodded, she asked, "Are
you going to the church picnic next weekend?"

"Yeah, I generally don't go, but I think it's time for me to get
out there a little more. I don't really fellowship all that much."

Monica smiled. "Have you looked into joining the singles group? We have a great group and we really get involved in so many things in the community."

I told her that I wasn't really keen on publicly announcing my desperation.

Monica laughed and said, "You need to try it out!"

I straightened out her account, and she thanked me and prepared to leave. Before she walked away she asked me to give her a call someday if I wanted to have coffee or something after the service. Her invite caught me off guard because women like Monica rarely even see me, let alone agree to be seen out in public with me. She was all gloss and sexiness. I must admit that I was really surprised that she was a member of Northrup. Monica had the sass of a woman who'd long ago decided that she'd rather be dead than a church girl.

Weeks passed, and no, I did not call Monica for coffee. Frankly, I felt that she was just being nice because I had corrected a $2,000 charge on her credit card. Some women can start off polite, but they usually stop when you don't get the message that they were just being nice to you when they gave you their number, let you buy them a drink, or danced with you all close. I'd been wrong many times and eventually developed a fail-proof system: if I was excited at the end of the night that a woman had connected with me, then she was just being polite. If I could care less if the woman and I saw each other again, then she was really interested.

Monica was definitely someone I wanted to get to know better, which meant that she was just being polite, and the last thing that I wanted was to become the church stalker.

A few days later a page came through at work for me to come out to the reception area. I was pissed because I usually like to have a name before I come out so that I know what I am getting into. Would it be Mr. Coyle still complaining that we'd charged him too much for his brakes? Was it Ms. Lynn with another excuse for why her latest check had been returned? It had been a really long week, and I was just looking forward to six o'clock and a calm ride home toward my uneventful weekend. I trudged up front, not sure what was going to meet me. Monica stood there with two cups of coffee and the most radiant smile.

"I am not really good on waiting. So, I decided to just bring the coffee to you," said Monica. I could not help smiling. Monica was in this tight red dress that wrapped around her body and made her look like the perfect number 8. It was cut low on her chest, and a huge medallion hung in between her breasts. She'd changed her hair. Her blond locks were pulled back into a knot behind her head and she just gleamed. The salesmen had stepped from behind their desks to get a better look, but sorry, bros, she was there to see me. With my ego on tilt I invited Monica into the lounge and we sat down for coffee.

Over coffee she told me that she was surprised that I hadn't called. "I am not the type to sit around wondering, so I took a chance that you'd still be here after I got off work."

"Well, my dog has been sick the last few weeks, and I have been real distracted here at work and all. I was going to call you at the end of the week," I explained lamely.

Monica rolled her eyes and said, "You are a clean brother, neat and in order. I seriously doubt you have a dog. However, I look forward to meeting Fido one day." She knew I was lying and was making light of it. "Bryce, no worries. I am aggressive, but I am not crazy. I just want to get to know you, but if you are involved I will back away."

"Definitely not involved," I said.

"Fine," she said. "The best way to get to know me is to attend the singles happy hour at the church tomorrow night." A happy hour at the church didn't make much sense to me, but if this woman really wanted to see me, then I was more than willing to try it out.

Saturday night I arrived at the church and was surprised at the number of cars in the parking lot. I walked up to the main church doors, and there was a sign that the singles happy hour was next door in the church's community center. When I walked into the center the room had been transformed. What was usually just a wide-open space used as a gym for the church school or overflow seating for services now had the vibe of a downtown club. There were plush red rugs all over the floor. The lights were dim and there were couches around the room. As I looked around I saw several bars spread about and heard jazz playing lightly in the background. The room was filled with women and men lounging on the couches or standing around the bars mixing it up. This was strange: a church building completely converted into one of the hippest lounges I'd ever seen. The only hints of its church roots were the scripture quotes hanging from the rafters.

I did not see Monica right away, so I felt out of place. Even though I had been a member of Northrup for two years, I didn't really know anyone else there. With more than ten thousand members, it was kind of a hard place to have that old-school family feeling, and anyway, what I really wanted was to get my spiritual food and keep it moving. When I was growing up, the churches I attended were smaller and warmer. We all knew one another, and there was a whole lot of getting into one another's business; from finances to funerals, there was so much drama. Northrup had none of that as far as I could see. Maybe there was some inner sanctum of ministers, employees, and high-level members who had the drama, but I was just a member bee who came to serve, pay my tithe, and leave. But here I was, wondering if I had made a mistake and should leave, when I heard someone call my name. I turned to see Monica walking up in the littlest black dress ever with another woman. Everything of interest was barely covered, yet Monica still looked classy because it seemed to fit so well. I could not help smiling when I saw her, and she quickly reached me and gave me a hug. "This is my friend Tonya," Monica said, and quickly shuffled me over to the VIP area of the lounge.

In the VIP area Monica showed me the bar, where every drink you could imagine was served in its nonalcoholic form with a biblical twist: Safe Sex, Wisdom in a Glass, One Spirit. I was a little confused by all of the choices and opted for a simple seltzer. Monica then led me over to a couch where Tonya was already sitting, while she went and made the rounds of the room hugging, kissing, running her fingers over the hair and backs of her friends. I was a little jealous of how intimate she was with this group and hopeful that she'd get just as familiar with me. Once I sat down, Tonya began to do the girlfriend drill. She was running interference, coming up with creative ways to ask me the same questions Monica had asked, and then checking to see if my answers were consistent. No, I had never been married. No, I did not have kids. Yes, I was born and raised in Baltimore. Yep, my parents had been married nearly fifty years. No, I hadn't finished up at Morgan. And yeah, I was pretty much the guy with whom what you see is what you get.

Monica made her way back over to the couch after the grilling and Tonya suddenly saw some people in the room that she needed to talk to—the universal sign that it was okay for Monica to proceed. I had passed the first test. Monica sat close to me and crossed her penny-colored legs. All night I had been trying to think of the perfect way to describe her skin, and the best that I could come up with was that it was the bronze shade only found in new pennies. Her blond hair cast a brilliance over her, like she had her own personal spotlight following her from room to room.

"You know, this was my idea," said Monica. "These happy hours were a hard sell to Pastor Blake, but I just knew that the congregation would love the idea of a lounge for the Lord."

"Lounge for the Lord—that is too original." I thought Monica was pushing with that one. "I am going to be honest—I didn't think that it would be all that interesting, but it is. You've created something unique, Monica. Judging by the crowd, people need this." Monica nodded and I thought I saw her blush for a brief second.

That night in between Monica sashaying away to greet others that she'd personally invited and making sure the DJ mixed in some neo soul with the jazz, Monica and I talked and got to know each other. "I had one of the worst marriages ever, but I am finally able to be cordial with my ex. He was a good guy married to the wrong woman, and we fought trying to force things to fit," said Monica. "I came to Baltimore when my job in Richmond transferred me up here. It was a welcome change after the divorce—a fresh start, you know." She'd bought and restored a row house in Patterson Park, and even she could not believe how at peace she was now that her career was thriving and she felt right at home in the city. "I joined Northrup because one of my co-workers kept inviting me, and once I joined it was the final piece of the puzzle for me: great city, great house, new friends, and now new fellowship." At Northrup Monica loved the diversity of the congregation: professionals next to laborers, straight on the same pew with gay, and young praising right along with the old. Monica felt that Northrup was the new model of church that could be accepting of all and still minister to the masses. Northrup was her high, and she just hoped that she would never grow tired of its buzz.

At the end of the night I knew that I wanted to see Monica again, and I fought my instincts on it—could she really be doing more than just being polite? She was the first undamaged woman I had met in a long time, and it was refreshing. Monica seemed to be genuinely interested in me and comfortable enough in her own skin to be at peace with me treating her well. I walked over to her while she was in the middle of a conversation with a group of guys and tapped her on the shoulder to say goodbye. Monica then introduced me to the group: "Bryce, this is Madison, Tonio, and Andre; they are my aces for planning singles events for the church." The brothers looked me up and down and then said a quiet hello. They clearly were not feeling the new guy in the room, and I felt like I'd interrupted something important. They kept their eyes on Monica as she pulled me over to the side to talk. Madison and Tonio linked arms and headed toward the bar, while Andre, without any shame, followed Monica's ass with his eyes as she walked off with me. She thanked me for giving the night a try. She said, "As you can see, we are not Bible-thumping losers, just like-minded people looking for an alternative to your typical scene."

"I get it, but let me tell you, there are a few losers in the room," I responded. Monica giggled and placed her index finger to her lips while nodding in agreement. There was the sister walking around in overalls and ponytails, and the brother who obviously did not know that a shower and a haircut were standard requirements for a night out. There were losers, but far fewer than you would get in a typical club. She gave me a hug goodbye and surprised me by giving me a quick kiss on the cheek.

"A getting-to-know-you kiss just for Bryce."

"I don't care what type of kiss that was. It was nice," I quickly tossed back.

"If you treat a sista right, you may get one of my famous good-morning kisses one day!" said Monica with a quick wink. We smiled at each other, and then she waved goodbye to me and went back to her friends.

It had been so long since I had been with anyone that the sensation of Monica's kiss, along with the image of her round firm tits, would not leave me. I couldn't sleep because my mind kept turning to her in that black dress and my dick stayed hard. Usually I could sleep thoughts of sex away or think about all of the work facing me in the morning, but none of those tricks worked for me that night. The only relief that I was going to get was manual, and so I started to jerk myself off. It was quick because it had been so long, but it was definitely worth it. It had been a while since a real woman's image had led me to release. Tonight it wasn't Gabrielle, Rihanna, or Sanaa—it was Monica.

The next morning I was in a mad rush to get ready for church. When I stepped out of the shower the message light on my phone caught my eye. Usually I would ignore it because I was running late—as was the case all week—but on Sundays my mom called to share her Scripture of the week. She called all four of her children each Sunday since we left home. When we were all young she gave it to us in person before we got in the car to go to church. For her—and for me—it wasn't just about the spiritual food, but more about the fact that she loved us and wanted us to know it.

I have always taken a lot of pride in the success of my family. My parents have been married forever, mostly happily, both had successful careers, and they managed to have four children that while diverse in their level of success never became a drain or disappointment to their parents. Mine was the successful black family that people want to say does not exist. They do exist, but there really is nothing about them that sells papers or make ratings for news shows. I always wanted what my parents have and often wondered if that was a realistic goal. Meeting Monica was making it seem a bit more likely.

I quickly went through my weekly hangers-on messages on my answering machine. Hangers-on were ladies that simply did not get the message that the relationship was over. There was Tiffany, who was just plain crazy; even after I blocked her phone number she continued to buy prepaid cell phones so that she could still get through. Oh, and I cannot forget Meshon, who told me that I was a "lame-ass soft dick" in the middle of the Towson Town Center food court, but who kept calling every few weeks to see if I wanted to come over. Hmmm, let's see—the answer would be no.

The next message was Mom with her verse—a good one on the power of perseverance. The final message opened up with a voice that I did not immediately recognize. "Bryce, it's Monica. I found your number in the church directory, and I just wanted to thank you for coming out last night. I didn't want you to think that I just stole a kiss and ran. Anyway, have a good day, and give me a ring when you get a moment." Monica was definitely putting the pressure on, and I thought, *This one is going to be fun.* Not call the most interesting woman I'd met in years? Never.

Over the next few weeks Monica and I really got to know each other with movies, plays, and dinners at our favorite restaurants. We even went biking. Look, half of this stuff I found boring, but being with Monica made it tolerable. Things were changing for me. No longer was I the average guy. Now I was the guy with the great girl. Monica was beautiful, smart, soulful, and funny. Other dudes were trying to figure out what she saw in me, and ladies were trying to get a piece just because someone else—a *gorgeous* someone else—wanted me. It felt amazing to be with a lady without constantly looking over her shoulder for the next best thing. Not to say that I still didn't look at other women, but now I'd only take a glance and then get right back to my lady.

We hadn't made our relationship status official, but I was starting to feel as if Monica was mine. We spent a lot of time together, including some of our nights. Now, these were "Christian nights," where we would both fall asleep on her couch, and later she would cover me with a blanket and give me a pillow and she would go into her bedroom to sleep—advanced sleepovers that offered no pressure but allowed us to feel close. We talked about sex, and Monica made it clear to me that she was not interested in playing games with me. She said she enjoyed sex but that it was important to her that a man appreciate being with her for all the right reasons. I got it. She wanted me to earn the right to be with her, and I was more than up to the challenge.

One night we were just lying on the couch watching one of the worst movies ever when Monica said, "I'm bored. Let's go to bed." I looked at her and said, "But I want to finish the movie. You can't suffer this long and not find out how it ends." I told her to just go ahead and throw me the blanket and pillow and that she could go ahead and go to bed. The next thing I knew her hair was inching its way up my leg. I turned, at first irked to be missing something in the movie, but then I noticed the tickle on my legs was not just the familiar feel of Monica's hair but the extra surprise of her skin. Monica stood up, naked from head to toe. Her body looked like one of those paintings from the medieval period, every curve clearly defined and full. Her satiny skin glistened, and damn, the girl was fully shaved—all things that I liked. Now, most dudes would have been up off the couch and on Monica in a second, but I hesitated. Did she really want to do this? Was she simply bored? Was this her way of not watching a bad movie? I was nervous because I knew that this was something that could either enhance or destroy the great thing we'd had going over the last few weeks.

I pulled Monica down on the couch next to me, and I let her know that the last few weeks had been great—just being around her and knowing that she wanted to spend time with me. Without pretense and with the most sincerity that I could put together, I broke down how I felt about her. "I'm not sure that I love you, but I know that I could one day. I care deeply for you, and I would never lie to you, and I don't want you to even think that this is not a heavy moment for me because it is." Monica deserved to know where I was with her and that it would be okay if she decided to not do this. I looked into her eyes for an answer and Monica stared intently back.

She ran her hands under my shirt and pulled it over my head, then ran her hands down my chest to my sweatpants. She softly rubbed my dick and said, "You seem excited, and I don't want to disappoint you." And with that she hopped from the couch and ran naked into her bedroom, her ass bouncing. I was never more thankful for having a "church freak."

Bryce Pierce was no longer a dullard of a man. I was getting it on the regular from one of the finest women in the city. I was no longer home all nights of the week or ducking the calls of ex-lovers. I had friends now, at work and at church, and since introducing Monica to my parents and siblings, I was no longer the only single person at family get-togethers. I had arrived into a world that I thought was only for others, filled with romance, passion, and hope for the future.

Sex did not change things much between Monica and me. We fell into an easy groove of sleepovers, experimentation, and play. For the first time I understood why some men marry. You meet someone that you enjoy and there is no pretense. It really was possible to have one person meet all of your needs, and Monica was that person for me.

The biggest discovery was just how much was out there sexually that I had never experienced. When Monica told me that she was opening herself up to me, she wasn't lying. Her night table was filled with toys that made me scream with delight and creams that made her call for God in a way I thought only the infirmed and insane could do. Monica wanted to try everything new and different, and I was her willing partner. It was nothing for us to have sex in her laundry room during the day when most residents were at work. We would pop in our favorite porn flicks to mix it up a bit. She was the first woman who actually was turned on by watching me please myself. She would talk dirty to me and pose sitting on top of her dresser. I could tell her what I wanted her to do to herself and she would just do it. It was better than any Net chat or film. One time I kind of got outside myself and told her to stick a finger in her pussy and her ass. She did it without hesitation. She never once questioned a request. Monica did it all, and I was totally satisfied.

We often played a game of "tell me your fantasy." It was a way for us to make sure that each of us was getting our needs met. I knew that Monica had probably gotten the idea from a book or magazine article somewhere with a title like "Ways to Always Get What You Want" or "Throw Your Man a Bone." I only did these things because they made her happy, and personally I reaped the rewards of all of her sexual scavenger hunts.

One night Monica asked me if I wanted to know one of her favorite fantasies. When I said, "Sure," she told me that she would love to watch me have sex with another woman.

"What?" I said.

"Really," she said. "I think you are so sexy, and I would love to just sit back and get off on watching you do your thing with someone else." I did not know what the "right" answer to this one would be. But when in doubt, offer up an alternative.

"Why don't we tape ourselves and then watch it back?" I suggested.

Monica quickly shot that down because she did not want to see herself on film and because she really wanted me to "star" in something for her—even if it was only a onetime image that she could treasure. I looked at her again and said, "Are you serious?" and could clearly see that this scenario was no joke. It was one of those once-in-a-lifetime moments where I could do the right thing and say no because it would ruin our relationship or I could seize the moment and get the fantasy with a partner willing to participate.

"Sure," I said to Monica. "If this is what you want . . . I am willing to try it out." My guess was that she would back out once she really thought about it, but Monica was pretty daring, so there was a chance we would see this fantasy through.

Many weeks passed, but Monica never brought up her fantasy of seeing me with another woman. I was a bit relieved not to have to think about that one. My fear was that on paper and in her mind it made sense, but once we were in the room she would not be quite as turned on by seeing me eat another woman out or having her call my name. We went back to our regular sexual play of late nights, early mornings, and everything in between. One day while I was at work I received an email invitation to a special edition of Northrup's singles happy hour that Saturday night. The invite said it was an exclusive event hosted by Monica. I'd been attending her singles events regularly since that first night and had really grown to enjoy them. Monica had a great group of friends who were starting to accept me as her man. I quickly clicked yes and commented that I would be there with "the hottest lady at Northrup."

Saturday came quickly, and I was definitely in weekend mode. Weekends now went like this for me: breakfast, workout, call Monica, meet for lunch, grab a movie, dinner with Monica, and back to one of our places for the evening until church on Sunday. I enjoyed everything but the workout. Working out was a new addition, so that I could simply keep up with Monica. She had so much energy and was extremely flexible. Monica loved to eat, which was great for me, but she also loved to burn it off through yoga, running, and sex—so a brother had to get up to speed real quick.

That day, our plans were a little different because I wasn't going to see her all day; we were going to meet that night at happy hour. The only time that I heard from her was when she called midday to say that she was thinking of me and could not wait to see me later. She said that she was incredibly horny and our small sexual break—her idea—was growing old. We did these breaks sometimes because Monica had read that they kept things fresh and broke up the routine. I didn't complain because Monica could rarely hold out the full week that she'd planned on; around day number two Monica would be ringing my phone trying to come over. This time she'd actually lasted the full week. I was anxious to see her as well, and I could not wait for happy hour to be over so that I could get in a bit of private time.

I arrived at the church about seven-thirty and walked over to the community center as usual. The windows were dark and it did not look like much was going on inside, if anything. I pulled the handle to the door and it did not move. Peering in the window, I saw dim lighting in some of the back offices, but nothing going on in the main room. I turned to look at the lot. There were several cars that I had recognized, including Monica's, but I didn't see anyone. I took out my cell and hit 5 for Monica, and she quickly answered. She told me that they were not in the usual spot—they had moved the happy hour over to the main church building. *Strange,* I thought; *why would they now hold it in the sanctuary portion of the building?* But I proceeded across the lot toward the church. I entered the large glass doors, and I saw some light coming from one of the side chapel rooms. The church used these mini-sanctuaries for smaller events such as baptisms, christenings, and discreet quickie marriages. Monica quickly popped out of the chapel and shut the heavy wooden door behind her. She leaned in and kissed my lips. Then she stepped back, gave me a once-over, and declared me "incredibly hot." I said a quick thanks and told her how stunning she was as well. She had on a purple tube dress that hugged every curve and a pair of black Louboutins that had taken me several paychecks to afford but were worth every dime; they made every aspect of her body jump to attention from her calves to her hips—even her nipples looked firmer, more tasty, and more desirable when she had on those shoes. I placed my hand behind her to open the door, but she grabbed the handle. I looked at her, wondering what was going on, and she leaned in and whispered, "Are you ready to have your every fantasy fulfilled?"

"Yeah," I answered, "but that will have to wait until after saved drinks with the single and sullen."

Usually Monica would laugh and tell me that I needed to stop hating, but she ignored my comment and once again asked, "Are you ready?"

Hell, I was ready for anything if it was going to get me into this room and eventually out of it with Monica on the way home to my bed. "Let's go," I said. "I am so ready for this night to both start and end."

Monica smiled at me and pulled me closer. She pressed her breasts into my chest, and even through my suit jacket, my dress shirt, and my T-shirt I could still feel her warmth. She tilted her head toward mine and gently bit my bottom lip. Monica then smiled at me and stepped backward to open the door.

The room was lit with amber light and scented with lavender. There were candles everywhere, and about ten people were sitting around on the floor on huge pillows. The pews that were normally in the chapel had been removed. There were a few more people standing around the room. Most were happy hour regulars, like Monica's friend Tonya and her boys Madison and Andre. Some were new to me and I'd never seen them before. The room had a strange aura of expectation, like they had been waiting for me to arrive. It was like that scene out of *Rosemary's Baby* where Rosemary finally gets to see her son; she enters the room and they all simply stare and greet her like they are all in on a secret that she has yet to uncover. We all know how badly that scene ended, and I was beginning to think this one was going to end the same way.

Monica led me to the middle of the room and removed my jacket. The lavender fragrance and her intoxicating scent were going to my head. She dropped my jacket on the floor and began to sway to the soft music playing in the room. She rubbed her hands up and down my arms a few times and then slowly began to unbutton my shirt.

I grabbed her hands and pulled her close to me to ask, "What are you doing?"

"Relax and go with it," she replied.

I wasn't relaxed, and I was tired of not knowing what was going on. When I finally looked around I noticed that the whole room had surrounded us in a circle, holding their drinks and taking in the main attraction: Bryce and Monica. Just when I was about to grab Monica's hand and go, the crowd parted and Monica's friend Tonya walked toward us naked except for her belly ring, which glistened in the darkness of the room. Generally, guys try not to notice their girl's friends, and for the most part I'd been successful with Tonya. Tonya had a pinched poodle face, and she needed some serious dental work done, but the one thing that you could not miss was Tonya's booty. She had the smallest waist and flattest stomach that appeared to explode into one of the fattest booties ever. Tonya had no face, hair, or breasts to speak of, but her booty was of such gigantic proportions that she'd broken many a saint's concentration when sliding by in the pew, crossing the front of the church to make announcements or serving up breakfast in between services. You could not miss Tonya. As I watched Tonya, things began to become clearer. I was to give my girl her fantasy tonight in God's house—in front of God's people.

Monica eased me down onto the floor. She then removed her dress. Tonya joined us down on the floor and sweetly and quite unexpectedly they shared a kiss. It was a strange sensation lying there watching them kiss. I did not know if I should be excited or a little scared. The two friends were kissing deeply, and Monica even let out a little moan when Tonya cupped her breast. Was this their first time? I wondered. Why were all of these people here gazing at this most private of shows? It was easy for a few moments to forget that we had an audience. I looked for a second away from Tonya and Monica and saw that our crowd was still tightly knit and taking it all in. Obviously there were some church socials that were quite sinister in nature.

Just when I was starting to think about all of the sexy get-togethers I might have missed over the years, the ladies turned their attention back to me. Monica ran her hands all over my body and played extra attention to the bulge in my pants. She kneaded my dick until it was so hard that I just knew I was about to burst through the fabric of my pants. The truth was that while I was just an average-looking brother, my dick was of monstrous proportions. I was a good twelve and a half inches and thick. Many women have run away from the challenge, but most, like Monica, loved to discover new ways to take me on. Sensing my need for freedom, Monica undid my pants and pulled them off. On her knees before me, she leaned in and slowly took my tip in between her lips. She sucked on it until it was taut and rock hard. Monica then took the full length of me into her mouth. The warmth of her mouth and smoothness of her throat engulfed me. She began to twist her lips and cup my balls, but I knew much more was coming, so I tightened up my mental game. I was not going to cum in her mouth when there seemed to be much more on the plate. All of a sudden Monica let out an "Ahhhhh" that seemed to work its way through her body. I was so caught up in my thing that I did not realize that while Monica was giving me head, Tonya was behind Monica laying out the sexiest tongue tease ever. My girl was getting eaten out by her best friend. This was no movie. This was really happening. Liquid was just oozing down between Monica's legs. My girl was enjoying herself, and on the real, so was I.

Monica then came up for air and removed the rest of my clothes. She wanted me to lie on my stomach flat on the floor. When I rolled over I was able to lift my head a little to check out the rest of the room. Our audience had splintered into groups settled down on the many pillows scattered throughout the room. Some couples had stripped down and were just watching, while in others the men had their dicks out while their women were sucking them off; my personal favorite were the ladies who were alone, their hands jammed down into their panties, pleasing themselves to our spectacle. Over in a candlelit corner I barely made out a threesome: Andre kneeling before his girlfriend, Rachel, playing with her clit while Madison was on his back under Andre licking his taint. I guess Tonio must have been home sick or something, but Madison appeared to be doing fine on his own. I had heard my boys talk about orgies, group sex, and the like, but for once I knew what it was like, and even the freakiest of them couldn't imagine such a thing in a church.

Just as I was taken away by the scene in front of me I felt a strange sensation. It was cold. Monica had spread her body out over my back. Her breasts were on my shoulders, her stomach on my lower back and her pussy on top of my ass. Tonya played with both of our asses. First it was a tongue, then a finger, and then a cold toy. Look, I am all dude, but a finger up the ass can at times be refreshing, and Monica knew that I did not mind getting down like that. Tonya worked the "icicle"—a frozen long glass anal plug—in both Monica and me. Sensing that I was getting more and more turned on, Monica jammed her hand underneath me and wrapped it around my dick and started jerking me to the rhythm of Tonya's penetration. These women were turning me out tonight, and I was more than willing to let this play out. When I thought things couldn't get any wilder, Monica flipped me over and said that it was time for her special treat. Tonya turned her body so her back was toward me and with her hand held all twelve and a half inches of me as she eased her big booty down onto my dick. Her booty was something to behold, perfectly round and the color of a roasted peanut, and I was cracking that nut tonight. Her pussy locked around my dick, and slowly she was able to take it all in. Tonya proceeded to bounce on my dick, and the craziness of her big booty and the firmness of her thighs and calves propelling her in this pursuit were pushing me to my limit. Monica was transfixed by what was playing out in front of her; she had one hand on my head rubbing it lovingly as she said, "Get yours, baby," and the other in between her legs getting herself where she needed to go. Monica orgasmed twice while Tonya was riding me. I saw her body shake and heard her telltale moan. My woman was enjoying herself thoroughly. She then turned to me and told me that she wanted to make me cum. With the little breath that I had left from Tonya's ever accommodating pussy I told her I wanted that too. She pushed Tonya off me and told me that it was only fair to slow things down and give Tonya what she needed, and with that my girl, the woman who had fulfilled all of my fantasies, placed her face down on Tonya's pussy. Tonya grabbed Monica's head and dug it down deeper into her; she wanted Monica to taste every inch of me in her. Tonya kept telling Monica, "I know how you like it," and that no dick could replace her. Tonya then yelled out something I did not quite understand and fell back onto the floor. Monica kissed her on the lips and came for me. She crawled on top of me and kissed me on the mouth. It was an intoxicating mix of Tonya's pussy and the warmth that I knew was all Monica. She slid her belly down on top of me and took me in. Monica rode me slowly just like I liked it and locked her fingers with mine. We were connected in that moment. She rocked her hips back and forth and then whispered into my neck, "Thank you, baby, for this . . . thank you, baby, for this." And then all of the excitement poured from my body. I held on to Monica so tightly, frightened that the spasms of my body would push her away from me. I came so hard that my head hurt. I held Monica as close as I could, in order to not let this moment get away. It was there in the chapel that I truly lost my virginity— the virginity of conventional thought when it came to sex and what it really means to be committed in a relationship.

It would not be the last time Monica and I would attend the special invitation-only church social. Religion really can be the glue for a successful relationship.

Destiny

Just Press Send

I finally get it. Love should feel good, warm and fuzzy. All the superficial stuff has been done away with because I want to be one with you. Looking for happily ever after wrapped up in the greatest friendship ever. I am ready for what I need in a man and hopefully I will get what I want. Are you my happy ending? TSOOO

The latest *TEASE* mixer was a success! Our clients came out in droves to meet other clients and get a close look at who makes the magazine run. The club was filled to the brim and I could not have been more excited. All of the positive buzz around the magazine could only increase circulation and ads, which meant bigger bonuses at the end of the year. My career was on fire, and I was thrilled.

Many hookups were made. Darwin and Lilly hit it off immediately, and from what I understand Lilly did not make it back to her place that night. She is finally getting her post-divorce groove on. Cassandra and Dave were all over Lilac checking out the scene, or rather, on the hunt. When I went out front for some air, there they were with one of the models we'd hired for the night, Dave rubbing the girl's shoulders and Cassandra out in the street desperately trying to grab a cab before the girl changed her mind. My ex-boyfriend Kennedy made it into town for the party. The ladies in the club were losing their minds over him, but he was a good boy just handing out flyers for his summer jazz festival on the water. Someone told me he'd met someone at school. I'll have to send him an email to get the details. The funniest thing of the night, though, was watching Jacob, drunk as hell, trying to make moves on Deanna. We'd convinced her after more than five years of working at *TEASE* to come out to one of the events. She fought us at first but then changed her mind when she found out that Platinum Parties was doing our gift bags and they included a mini spa vacation in each bag. She had to come to the party to get a bag, though, and so Deanna was in the house. She'd sexed it up a bit with a nice little black dress and had let her hair fall in soft waves down her back. After five Deanna reminded me of Lynn Whitfield from *Eve's Bayou*—all class and understated sexy. Jacob had Deanna trapped on a couch in the VIP area and was trying real hard to get close. If the boy breaks her, he really is the lothario he says he is!

The night was a magical one, and I am so proud of the work that I do at *TEASE*. The teasers in the room that night were a really different bunch, with all of their lovelorn stories, secret passions, and off-the-charts desires, but they were bold enough to go out and get what they wanted. I was Mama Love Bug that night, proud that I was giving them what they needed.

My personal life? Not quite so fulfilling. After the fiasco of Denae I decided to take a bit of a break from dating. I had to get my head on straight and really decide what I was doing. Did I want to just mix it up and date? Was I looking to settle down?

Was all of it pointless because I was destined to be alone? After several nights of girlfriend phone conferences, huddling with relationship guides, and just staring stupidly into my bathroom mirror (don't knock it till you've tried it), it came to me that what I wanted was a brother who loved and excited me.

Denae had been able to pull me in because his sex appeal was intoxicating, but he was a horrible person. Josh was a nice guy, but not exciting enough to hold my attention for longer than a few hours. I needed some superhero type who combined the best of both guys for my ultimate satisfaction. Denae's dick with Josh's brain, Josh's consideration with Denae's hint of danger—that's what I needed.

I called Josh to apologize for my behavior, and he accepted. He explained to me that he'd known that I wasn't feeling him and that it was okay. I was about to invite him out for coffee, but he told me that it was actually good that I'd passed on him because he was seeing someone new and things were really working out. *Sigh*. I was too late for Josh, but it was cool to finally let down my guard with him and let him know that he was a good guy and that I was the bad girl because I could not see it all those months ago. We got off the phone promising to stay in touch and knowing that that would be the last time we'd speak.

A few days later Katina came bouncing into my office at the end of the day talking about how her man had asked her to move in with him and she did not know what to do. She loved him and things were good, but she was scared to commit too early. I told Katina my truth: that I had let too many good ones slip through my fingers because I'd been scared of what *might* happen. If this guy was the reason she'd been beaming the last few weeks, then clearly he was worthy of some sort of commitment. Katina said he was definitely one of the great ones and she'd consider moving in. I walked her to the door and watched her run across the street . . . into the arms of Josh. Katina hugged him and held his hand as they walked down the block. Josh's face lit up when he saw her, and Katina was glued to his side. They were a perfect fit and I wasn't jealous of them. Their happiness in that moment gave me hope that I could one day find my fit.

I went back to my computer and opened up my email. There were several messages from my brother Tonio with "Madison has fucked up again" in the subject line. *These two really need to chill,* I thought. Weren't they doing some sort of couples therapy at church to slow down the drama? I was about to open my latest teaser submissions when it occurred to me, *What the hell am I waiting for?* In my saved drafts I found my much-delayed personal ad and I hit send. It was time to hook Destiny up.

Acknowledgments

It has been two years since my last book, and there are so many people who have been instrumental in keeping me sane. First off, I want to thank my listeners at 92Q and the readers of my books, columns, and articles. You have all been so encouraging and open with me, and it is truly a pleasure stepping into your relationship worlds every day. Thanks to my team of V. Sanders, M. Guy, and P. Burke for challenging me and forcing me to grow and evolve as a writer. Huge thanks always go out to my parents, the Wrays, for providing the groundwork for me to even think a career in writing was possible. Then there is my guy in NYC, my brother, Lamont—thanks for letting a married gal get a little wild with you on the weekends. Thanks for being the best brother ever, but more importantly my friend. Then there is the best home team ever—JB and Alec. Thanks for making it easier for me to do this by allowing me to be wife, mom, and diva!

LaDawn Black, a native of Washington, D.C., is a relation-ship expert, radio personality, and author of two previous books, *Stripped Bare* and *Let's Get It On*. *TEASE* is her first work of fiction.

Five nights a week she hosts Baltimore's number one radio relationship show, "The Love Zone" on 92Q (92.3 FM). Black is a relationship coach for match.com, essence.com, and blackmeninamerica.com, and has contributed to or been profiled by *Essence, Ebony, Glamour, Men's Health, Cos-mopolitan,* and the *Washington Post,* among others.

Black was named Best Radio Personality by the *Baltimore City Paper* and Best Guilty Pleasure Radio Show by *Baltimore Magazine* and was nominated for Urban Radio Personality of the Year by *Radio and Records* magazine. She currently resides in Baltimore with her two very best men, JB and Alec.

www.ladawnblack.com